When Hailey Met Mac...

Eight years ago we shared one long, hot kiss. *Big deal, one kiss,* you're probably thinking. But check him out on the front cover—a kiss from a man as sexy as he is.... Anyway, Mac ended up marrying another woman and having a baby girl. I married a single dad and doted on his little kids. And I figured Mac forgot about that kiss.

He didn't. But now that we're both single, we're not exactly rushing to the altar. Okay, *he's* not exactly proposing marriage. But we are sharing much more than just hot kisses....

Dear Reader,

Here I am, your new correspondent. I admit to having been a little nervous as to what I might say in this letter, but then I started thinking about this month's books, and Lass Small's *The Case of the Lady in Apartment 308* got me thinking. What it specifically got me thinking about was my own house, which I own. Well, okay, the bank and I own it—and I bet you can guess whose is the larger share. Anyway, the thing is, I've started to think it might be nice to rent, not own. That thought first occurred to me after I fell down the stairs with the lawn mower. (Don't ask.) Then there was the night—early morning, really: 2:00 a.m.—I nearly electrocuted myself trying to turn off the attic fan. (Don't ask about *that,* either.) And then I read about Ed Hollingsworth, and now I'm sure of it: If I can have a landlord *just like him,* I'm putting my house on the market and renting from here on out!

After you finish falling in love with Ed, check out Celeste Hamilton's *When Mac Met Hailey.* It's equally delightful, the story of a man looking for…what? A wife? A mother for his daughter? Or just a hot date? Whichever it is, he finds her in Hailey Porter. Don't miss it.

See you next month—hopefully with no more housing traumas to report. Until then, enjoy!

Leslie Wainger
Senior Editor and Editorial Coordinator

Please address questions and book requests to:
Silhouette Reader Service
U.S.: 3010 Walden Ave., P.O. Box 1325, Buffalo, NY 14269
Canadian: P.O. Box 609, Fort Erie, Ont. L2A 5X3

CELESTE HAMILTON

When Mac Met Hailey

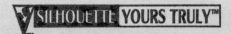

Published by Silhouette Books

America's Publisher of Contemporary Romance

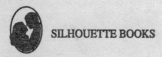

SILHOUETTE BOOKS

ISBN 0-373-52024-7

WHEN MAC MET HAILEY

Printed in U.S.A.

About the author

CELESTE HAMILTON

I couldn't be happier that my nineteenth novel for Silhouette Books is for the Yours Truly line. Why? Because these books are loads of fun, and writing this one has been a huge pleasure.

It's not that I didn't adore writing my other novels for Silhouette Special Edition and Desire. I plan to write lots more! But I also love the tone that's been set for Yours Truly. These are sassy and decidedly contemporary stories about modern couples with complex lives and problems who still manage to forge meaningful relationships. While this premise is the core of every satisfying romantic read, Yours Truly's plotlines have a unique and playful twist— the written communication that brings the hero and heroine unexpectedly together.

In my book, a half-forgotten notation in the hero's old "Little Black Book" draws Mac Williams and Hailey Porter back together. It's a fun beginning for the romance between two people who think they *aren't* looking for love. I hope reading Mac and Hailey's story brings as much enjoyment to you as writing the book brought to me.

Though I've been a waitress, a clerk, an advertising copywriter and a producer, I always knew I was supposed to be writing romantic, uplifting stories. Exactly the sort of stories that Silhouette publishes and you read! I thank them and you for making my dreams come true.

With warmest regards,

Celeste Hamilton

For Erica Spindler,
a wonderful writer and friend
whose support is an invaluable part of my life

Prologue

—→ ←—

"Thanks, this was fun." The simple phrase, an end-of-a-date standard, felt inadequate as Hailey Porter turned to face her escort.

"I had a great time, too." Mac Williams stepped close enough for her to feel his warm breath in the frosty January air.

"I'm glad."

They'd had dinner and planned on a movie. And talked. And laughed. And looked at each other. Long, approving looks. Warm, special looks. The heat between them was so palpable, Hailey had suggested they walk. Yet even a cold New York City night hadn't cooled the glow they were generating.

Now, here they were, in front of her building. Should she ask him up? She knew where that would lead. Though no prude, she was traditional enough, cautious enough, to hesitate. This was their first date. They had met only yesterday.

"It's late," she said, letting her regret show.

He exhaled. "And you've got a plane to catch to-morrow."

"At eight."

"So..." Mac stepped closer. His voice dropped lower. A streetlight picked up the tawny highlights in his hazel eyes. "Call me when you get back."

"Okay." Her heart began to pound.

He lifted a hand to the point where her blond hair skimmed the collar of her coat. "I guess this is goodnight."

He kissed her then. With none of the usual first kiss hesitation, none of the tentative questing or gentle probing she might have expected. This kiss was hot. Hard. Heavenly. She melted into the caress, uncharacteristically wishing she were another sort of woman, the kind who could take this virtual stranger's hand and lead him up to her bed.

He pulled away, finally, with a murmured, "Damn."

"Yes," she echoed. "Damn."

Releasing her, he stepped back. "Good night, Hailey."

She smiled, turned and walked up the stairs to her apartment lobby, careful not to look back lest he see the stars in her eyes. No matter how he had kissed her, it was still just a first date. She had to be cool. Once inside, however, she ran up four flights of stairs.

"You look pleased with yourself."

Choosing not to comment, Mac hung his overcoat and blazer in the closet by his apartment door.

Greg St. Clair, Mac's friend since the ninth grade and now his roommate, laughed. "I know that look. You got lucky."

Instead of answering, Mac began to whistle and made his way across the living room to the shabby fold-out couch that doubled as his bed.

Greg trailed him. "So the blonde was hot, huh?"

"Nice, too."

"Nice?" Frowning, Greg knotted the belt of the faded flannel robe he wore over his sweats. "How nice?"

"Interesting." Mac took off his tie and hung it over the arm of a floor lamp along with the others that were draped there.

"So you *didn't* get lucky."

"I had a great time."

Greg's opinion was expressed in one succinctly profane word.

Mac laughed at his buddy's comical disappointment, then went to the desk beside the couch and pulled his wallet from his pocket. A card fell out. Hailey's card, he realized, plucking it off the floor. Grinning, he sat down at the desk and pulled his address book toward him. This "little black book" was a stupid game he and Greg had started in college and only halfheartedly kept up now, some three years after graduation.

Well aware of Greg peering over his shoulder, Mac flipped to the P section and wrote down Hailey's name and phone number. To the side, he added, "One hot number." For emphasis he circled the phrase with a red pen he found on top of one of the many sketch pads Greg had lying around the place.

His friend whistled. "And she was just nice, huh?"

"Very nice."

"Give me details."

Mac rebuked him with a glance. "Grow up, St. Clair."

"Hey, I'm experiencing a personal dry spell. I need vicarious thrills."

"Then turn on the TV. We've got cable."

Greg stared at him for a moment. "Jeez, you must like her."

"Yep."

"You made another date?"

"She's leaving town. The public relations firm she works for is handling a publicity tour for the author of a big, new book. Hailey will be working on that, then she's going to visit her family in California. She'll be back in a month."

"A month?" Greg repeated. "Anything can happen in a month. If this chick is primed and ready, get back over to her place."

"I'd rather let the anticipation build."

"She'll be yesterday's news in a month."

"Not this woman," Mac said with confidence.

Disgusted, Greg went back to his room.

Mac flipped his address book closed and went to bed thinking of Hailey's kiss, of how wrong Greg was.

But he was right. Anything could happen in a month. It was just enough time to meet someone else, fall in love and retire your little black book for good.

1

The bed feels strange.

That was all Mac could think as he flung an arm toward his beeping alarm clock. He didn't reach the clock, and when he opened his eyes to look for it, the morning sun blinded him. That was stranger still. Because his and Eve's bed didn't face a window. Eve hated sunshine in her face before her morning coffee.

But Eve isn't here.

That thought jolted Mac awake, much like most of the mornings of the past two years. Eve was gone. And as for the bed, it felt strange because it was as new and unfamiliar to him as the rest of this room.

New bed. New room. New life.

Groaning, Mac sat up and silenced the clock. Then he looked around at the spacious dimensions and floor-to-ceiling windows of his new bedroom. A room like this was a find in Manhattan, the real estate agent had said.

"I hate it," Mac said. "I want to go home."

The words were no sooner out of his mouth than the door crashed open and a small figure did a half gainer into the center of the bed. Mac dodged his five-year-old daughter's lethal, flying arms and legs and looked up at the woman who stood in the doorway.

He hitched the sheets farther up his boxer-clad hips. "Good Lord, Phoebe, can't you give a guy his privacy?"

His sister-in-law glared at him. "MacKenzie Williams, that alarm's been going off for at least five minutes, and Julianna and I have been up and dressed for an hour."

Julianna bounced up and down, her red curls bobbing under a neat blue bow that matched her denim overalls. "Aunt Phoebe says we've got to whip this place into shape today."

"Isn't that what we did until about three this morning?"

Mac waited for the disapproving grunt he knew was coming from Phoebe.

"Half your life is still in boxes," she told him.

"I was thinking about leaving it that way. Julianna and I can just unpack as we need stuff."

Phoebe didn't bother to comment on that suggestion. She stalked off, her slim shoulders straight beneath her long white T-shirt. A red leather belt cinched the shirt in at her waist, large gold hoops swung at her ears, and black leggings completed her ensemble. Trust Phoebe to be fashionable for any and every occasion.

Mac exchanged a knowing look with his daughter.

"She made an egg thing," Julianna told him.

"Quiche?"

The little girl made a face. "I just had cereal. She said the egg thing was for everybody else. And she made that coffee that smells good."

Mac sighed. Phoebe was turning the gang's usual Sunday brunch into an occasion. She owned and operated a catering and party planning service. For Phoebe, life was one long event.

When the doorbell rang, Julianna gave Mac a hurried kiss and then scurried off. The voices of Mac's assistant, Sylvia, and his best friend, Greg, filtered down the hall before Mac closed the bedroom door and headed for a quick shower. In his *new* shower in his *new* master bath. Another plus, the real estate agent had said. An updated bathroom, just right for a couple. Mac could still remember the way the agent had thrown the shower door open, and the suggestive note in her voice as she had urged him to look at the spaciousness of the black-and-white tiled compartment. Mac had to wonder, were real estate agents now instructed to sell condos by pointing out the places where people could have sex?

Not that he might ever have sex again. As he stepped under the warm, well-modulated spray, he muttered, "I've sunk every dime I ever saved into a condo that has a couples' bathroom. And I'm not a couple."

If he'd had time, Mac might have given in to the melancholy that swamped him. For the two years since Eve had been gone, he had held the loneliness at bay by staying busy. There was Julianna, first and foremost, then his demanding job as producer of a top-rated radio talk show, and then his three closest friends, who were right now waiting to share a first Sunday brunch with him in his new home. A home they had urged him to buy.

"To get away from the constant reminders of Eve," Phoebe had said.

"You need to move on," Greg had urged.

"It's time," Sylvia had added.

All their clichéd phrases were right, Mac told himself. And if not, then this was one very expensive experiment.

He finished his shower, toweled off and found comfortable jeans and an old T-shirt in the first box he opened. He was smiling when he walked into the small but sun-splashed kitchen and dining area. The oak table set with china, crystal and cloth napkins gave evidence of Phoebe's handiwork. She and Julianna and the others were clustered at the glass doors that opened onto a tiny terrace overlooking a correspondingly small courtyard. Leaves of orange and gold fell from the trees that thrived there despite the building that enclosed them on three and a half sides. The pleasant, early October breeze brought the ever-present scents of the city to mingle with the more delicious aroma of one of Phoebe's famous quiches.

Greg, tall and lean, his shaggy dark hair worn in the same careless style he had first adopted in high school, turned from the doorway. "Jeez, Mac, I don't remember seeing the courtyard when I looked the place over with you."

"And it has a fountain." Gamin-faced Sylvia sighed dreamily. "I just love the sound of a fountain."

Phoebe cocked her sleek auburn-haired head to the side. "All I hear is traffic."

"Use some imagination," Greg instructed her. "You do have an imagination, don't you, Phoebe-baby?"

"Imagination," Phoebe mused. "Isn't that what people like you use to avoid getting real jobs?"

"Now, now," Mac cut in before the two could become embroiled in one of their infamous war of words. "No fights during this apartment's inaugural brunch."

"What's 'naugral?" Julianna asked.

"The first," Sylvia explained, hunkering down beside the little girl. "And if Aunt Phoebe and Uncle Greg don't fight, this will be an inaugural occasion for that, too."

Everyone laughed, even the two in question. Greg and Phoebe had known each other ever since Mac's whirlwind romance and marriage to Eve nearly eight years ago. Greg was an ex-hockey player turned cartoonist, with a suitably scatter-shot approach to life. And Phoebe was simply perfect. At everything. The combination had made for some interesting conversations over the years.

Julianna, who had already eaten, asked to be excused to go arrange stuffed animals in her new bedroom. She left and Sylvia suggested they have brunch. Then, touching a hand to her rounded hip, she groaned. "I shouldn't eat. I promised myself I wouldn't eat."

Mac pulled out a chair and dropped a kiss on his assistant's button nose just before she sat. "Sylvia, you're perfect just as you are."

"I don't think my date last night would agree."

Phoebe expertly lifted a slice of quiche onto a plate and passed it to the other woman. "What date?"

"The blind date with the cop I told you about."

"You're dating a cop?" Greg asked, sitting down and accepting a plate from Phoebe.

"It was one date." Sylvia rolled her eyes and handed the juice pitcher to Mac just as he took his seat.

Greg scooped a croissant from a basket and passed it on. "But with a cop? Isn't that a little mainstream for you, Sylvia? What's happened to your usual out-of-work actor, boyfriends?"

The talk swirled around Mac. Familiar and comforting, it took the lingering strangeness out of being in new surroundings. If he closed his eyes, this might be three years ago and Eve might be seated beside him. They would probably be having muffins, because Phoebe had been into whole grain about then, but everything else would be the same. The same good friends, the same china he and Eve had received as a wedding gift, the same pulpless orange juice she had liked. All just the same...

"Mac?"

He jerked his head up to find three pairs of eyes trained on him. "What?"

Greg cleared his throat. "You're zoning on us, man."

"Sorry." Mac forced a smile and dipped a fork into his untouched quiche. "I guess I was thinking about something else." He watched a look go around the table.

As usual, Phoebe was the one to take charge. "We've been talking, Mac—"

He held up a hand to cut her off. "Stop right there. The last time you guys talked, I wound up buying this place."

Sylvia touched his arm. "We think you need to start dating."

"Get back in the saddle," Greg added.

"And I know a lovely girl," Phoebe said with a smile.

They were so predictable, Mac thought. For the past year they had been using this routine on him. At least now he had a new excuse. "I think getting settled into this place is enough of a change for me and Julianna to handle right now."

Phoebe leaned forward, her expression intense. "But it's the perfect time to forge ahead."

"Why?"

"Because you're starting over," Sylvia stated pointedly.

Chuckling, Mac reached for the coffee carafe. "If that's the case, I might as well get new friends, too."

Greg looked uncharacteristically solemn. "Hey, we're not kidding. You need to get back out there. You're going to turn old before your time if you don't..." He shot a look at the two women. "It's not natural, you know. A guy has pressures—"

"Oh, please spare me," Phoebe cut in, glaring at Greg. She turned back to Mac. "We just want to see you happy."

"Relieving some pressures will make him happy," Greg argued. "If you two ladies will just leave this to me. I've been dating this girl and she has a friend—"

"And I bet she's a gem," Phoebe muttered.

Greg turned defensive. "This is a perfectly nice girl."

Sylvia chimed in. "We were going to set Mac up with my cousin Leeza from Jersey."

"Were we?" Phoebe's grimace marred her perfect forehead. "I thought it was my friend—"

"This girl—" Greg began.

"And my cousin—" Sylvia added.

"Hold it!" Mac didn't realize he had shouted until his friends turned startled faces toward him. It was then that he also realized he was angry. He was tired of having this same discussion every few weeks. Taking a second to steady himself, he held up a hand when Phoebe started to speak. "Just stop it. I appreciate the concern, but—"

"Mac, please listen to us," Sylvia began.

"Another word and I'm firing you," Mac retorted, only half in jest.

Everyone fell silent again.

Mac took a long swallow of the coffee he had poured, then faced the concerned trio around the table. "I really do appreciate you guys. Julianna and I wouldn't have made it this last year and a half without you. After Eve..." He paused to swallow. "Well...you all saved our lives. I think you were right about us moving. It probably will help us get on with our lives. But this stuff about dating...well, I'm not ready."

Three "buts" rang out before Mac silenced his friends once more with a glare. "I'm not ready," he repeated in a steely tone.

"You've been saying that for a year," Phoebe said.

"Then maybe I mean it." Mac sent Greg a hard look. "And if I were ready, I wouldn't need your girlfriend's bimbo buddy."

"She's not a bimbo," Greg protested rather weakly.

"And I'm not interested in your cousin Leeza," Mac told Sylvia. "Isn't she the one who breeds poodles? You know I hate poodles."

Sylvia flushed. "She's such a darling girl."

"Yeah, right," Mac muttered skeptically. Then he nailed Phoebe before she could say anything more. "I don't want to meet any of your picture-perfect friends, either."

She sniffed. "Well, if you don't want our help..."

"Thank you, I don't." Mac picked up his fork once again. "Now let's eat, shall we? And then you can all help me unpack the boxes of books in the living room."

There was a moment of silence. Another look was passed among the three coconspirators.

Then Greg picked up the conversational ball. "Tell me, Phoebe-baby," he drawled. "You got any friends you want to fix me up with?"

With a sweet smile, she replied, "My friends only date within their species."

"You guys," Sylvia admonished.

But Phoebe and Greg were off, swapping good-natured insults while Sylvia attempted to referee. Mac sat back, enjoying the familiar camaraderie that endured throughout the day. After brunch, the four adults, with Julianna's encouragement, unpacked crates, arranged books and bric-a-brac, hung pictures and debated furniture arrangements. Under Phoebe's strict supervision, work progressed rapidly. Late that evening, the place had taken on a semblance of hominess. Everyone was gone, Julianna was asleep, and one lone carton stood unpacked beside the computer desk in the alcove Mac planned to use as his home office.

Yawning, he thought about putting it off. Then Phoebe's disapproving expression rose in his mind and he plunged ahead. The first item that came out of the carton was an address book. His old little black book. He chuckled, wondering where this damn thing had been hiding for the past eight years. He didn't remember packing it, but that was no surprise since he'd thrown everything in this box in about ten minutes flat. Well, this was one thing that could go, he thought, and started to toss it aside.

Curiosity stopped him, made him open the book. Amusement kept him flipping the pages. Had he really dated all these girls and women? Eventually he reached the P section.

Hailey Porter. One hot number.

The memories came back. A clear, cold night. A kiss warm as whiskey, twice as intoxicating. Mac remembered long, blond hair. A pretty smile. The sort of legs a man dreams of slipping between.

His body stirred at the thought. The sensation was pleasantly welcome. Like a good friend, gone too long without visiting.

Hailey Porter. God, he had liked her.

If Hailey had called him after her trip, Mac didn't remember. He and Eve had met the weekend after Hailey had left, and fallen immediately head over heels in love. Everything had happened so fast. At the end of the month, they were engaged and planning a wedding. Then they eloped, throwing her family into a tizzy. Poor, proper Phoebe had been so angry, her plans for the perfect wedding dashed. But Eve had laughed at her, in just the way Eve always laughed . . .

Mac looked down at the address book again. And amazingly, he remembered Hailey's laugh, not Eve's. He remembered because Hailey's laugh had been so distinctive. Not loud, but full-throated. With a little nervous edge. Her laugh had been the first thing he'd noticed eight years ago when she had come into the television studio where he had been working as a production assistant. She had been young, even younger than his own twenty-four, but with a maturity that had surprised him. She had handled her firm's client, a nervous author making a first appearance on a nationally televised show, with aplomb.

Hailey had told Mac that family connections had brought her the job with the PR firm, but she had been determined to make it on her own merits. She'd been excited about handling the publicity tour of that author. Mac had liked her enthusiasm, liked everything about her. Especially the way she had kissed.

But then he had met Eve.

Setting the address book on the desk, Mac leaned back. Over his desk Phoebe had hung one of Eve's paintings. Her signature bold strokes had fashioned a flower vendor's stall overflowing with color. The image made Mac smile. Seeing the picture here, rather than in the apartment he had shared with Eve, meant he could enjoy it without the usual pang of sadness.

Maybe Phoebe, Greg and Sylvia were right. Maybe it was time to move on.

Or move back.

To Hailey Porter.

He laughed at the foolish notion. A woman like Hailey, lovely and full of intelligence and life, couldn't be unattached. And even if she were, how would he find her? Ambitious as she had been, she certainly wasn't still an assistant at the same PR firm she had worked with eight years ago.

But maybe they'll know where she is.

That thought flashed into Mac's head just before he closed the address book and shoved it in a drawer. Unfortunately, the thought couldn't be set aside so easily. He kept stepping over it the next morning while he took Julianna to school, while he met with his boss about topics for a week's worth of programs, and while they taped the nine-to-noon show.

Finally, at midafternoon, he punched in the number that had stuck in his brain like glue. The receptionist answered with a crisp, "Jenkins, Porter and Witherspoon Public Relations."

Porter. Maybe that meant Hailey Porter.

"May I help you?" the voice on the phone repeated.

Mac asked for Hailey, then held on, surprised by the way his palms had begun to perspire.

"Mac Williams on line three, Ms. Porter."

The intercom message startled Hailey. For a moment, all she could do was stare at the phone.

"Ms. Porter?" her receptionist, Dolores, queried.

Hailey cleared her throat. "Tell him I'll call back." She felt stupid, putting him off. But hearing his name like that, out of the clear blue, had rattled her. Mac Williams was nothing to her, but she didn't want to speak with him cold.

The chicly dressed, fortyish brunette seated opposite Hailey looked surprised. "Isn't Mac Williams the producer of The Day Varner Show?"

"I believe so," Hailey replied to her friend and associate, Pam Witherspoon.

"He probably wants Newton to be on the show."

Of course Mac was calling about a client, Hailey told herself. Clive Newton, a political writer with a controversial book about post-Cold War world poli-

tics currently climbing the bestseller lists, was the most
likely client on their firm's list to arouse Mac's interest. Pam was handling Newton's media appearances
to promote the book.

"Do you think Newton would agree to an interview with Varner? It might be interesting to hear
Newton match wits with an old-line liberal." Hailey
glanced up when Pam didn't answer.

"I wonder why you got the call from Williams instead of me?" Pam mused, frowning. "I hope Dolores isn't misdirecting calls again."

"Well, you can call him back."

"Why didn't you talk to him?"

"Because we're working."

Arching one slender eyebrow, Pam surveyed the remains of their late lunch, which was spread across the
low, glass-topped table between her chair and the love
seat where Hailey sat. Not commenting on the obvious, however, she just leaned over, pressed a button on
the phone and got Mac's number from Dolores. She
punched it in, asked for him, switched the phone to
speaker, and sat back.

A moment later his deep, pleasant voice poured
from the speaker phone. "Ms. Witherspoon, thanks
for getting back with me, but I called your firm looking for Ms. Hailey Porter."

Smoothly, Pam replied, "Yes, but since I'm in
charge of most of our client's media bookings..."

There was a short hesitation. Hailey heard what
sounded like papers rattling in the background. "I

wasn't calling about a booking. This was a personal call for Ms. Porter."

Pam's mouth formed an O. Hailey's stomach clenched.

"I'll call back," Mac continued.

"No," Pam said quickly. "Don't do that. She'll be right with you." Hitting the Hold button, she looked at Hailey.

There was no way Hailey could put him off again, but she clicked off the speaker before picking up the receiver. It was bad enough that Pam was watching her with such frank curiosity. Hailey didn't need her listening in to everything that was said on both ends.

"Hi, Mac," Hailey said into the phone, projecting what she hoped was a perfect blend of friendliness and professionalism. "How are you?"

Again he hesitated for a moment. "I wasn't sure you'd remember me."

"Of course I do. What's up?"

"I just, uh, I was going through some things and I ran across your name."

"You did?"

"Yes...and... well, I was wondering..." He cleared his throat, sounding, of all things, nervous. "I was hoping you might want to have...lunch."

"Lunch?" Hailey repeated before she could stop herself. Pam's eyebrows shot halfway up her forehead.

"Tomorrow? Maybe?"

"Let me check my book," Hailey prevaricated. "I think I'm busy tomorrow." To Hailey's chagrin, Pam shot over to the desk and grabbed the appointment book with Road Runner-like speed. One long, red-tipped nail bored into the empty space in the lines next to tomorrow's lunch hour.

"Then Wednesday perhaps?"

As if she knew what he had asked, Pam had flipped over to the day in question and was now pointing frantically at that equally empty line. Hailey was afraid her friend would scream out loud if she turned Mac down. "Wednesday, then."

He breathed an obvious sigh of relief, named a little French café Hailey knew, and they agreed to meet at one.

"I'm looking forward to seeing you again," he said in closing.

"Me, too. Goodbye."

The phone was barely back in its cradle before Pam squealed, "You hold-out! Since when do you know Mac Williams personally? This is a great connection. The Day Varner Show is hot, and everyone says the reason is his producer."

Hailey ran her fingers through her chin-length shag and shrugged with elaborate unconcern. "Is it so unlikely that I would have met him at some media function or the other?" she lied.

"If that were so, why did you let me call him back?"

"I really thought he was calling about Newton." Hailey began gathering up the half-empty cartons from their lunch. "Do you want this other egg roll?"

"No, and stop changing the subject."

"I'm not." Hailey crunched into the cold but still crispy roll, then took a dumpling from another carton. She looked up to find Pam studying her with suspicion. "What?" she mumbled around a mouthful of food.

"Something's up. You're stuffing your face, and you only do that when you're nervous."

Hailey swallowed. "Don't be silly. Mac Williams asked me to lunch. I'm going. You're always after me to accept invitations from men. So I'm going. I haven't seen him in nearly eight years, he may be gross now but—"

"Eight years?" Pam cut in. "You've known him for eight years?"

"No, I knew him—briefly—eight years ago."

Salacious interest aroused, Pam pounded. "You *knew* him? You mean, you guys had an affair?"

"Is everything sexual to you?"

"No, unfortunately, I've almost forgotten what sex feels like."

Hailey made a sound of disgust, tossed the uneaten portion of her egg roll aside and finished cleaning up their lunch, all the while avoiding Pam's intense regard. Silence stretched between them. The air was so thick with questions that Hailey finally broke under their weight. "All right, I'll tell you," she said, turning back to her friend.

Pam rubbed her hands together.

"It isn't juicy. We only had one date."

"A one-night stand." A look of horror replaced the keen interest on Pam's face. "Oh, God, Hailey, do you think this is one of those lunches that people set up with all the people they've ever slept with to tell them they have AIDS?''

"I didn't sleep with him."

"But maybe he thinks you did."

"I would hope he'd remember."

"You know how men can be," Pam continued. "We women can remember what we were wearing the first time the guy we liked in fifth grade smiled at us, but guys forget the names of women they spend whole weekends with."

Hailey pressed fingers to her throbbing temples. "Well, no matter what, I only kissed Mac Williams."

"How was it?"

"Pam!"

"I think that was a fair question," the brunette replied defensively. "I'd tell you."

"What makes you think I remember after almost eight years?"

Pam just looked at her.

Releasing a long sigh, Hailey sprawled back down on the love seat. "It was a wonderful kiss, a wonderful date. One of those where you hang on to each other's words."

"I had one of those," Pam murmured, crossing her arms and leaning back in her chair. "It was a long time ago, but I still have a vague recollection."

For once, Hailey let the other woman's poor-dateless-me routine go unremarked. She was remembering that night with Mac. "He blew me away. Completely."

"So what happened?"

The magical memories evaporated as Hailey recalled the long, difficult publicity and book-signing tour with the temperamental author. They were gone for weeks, then Hailey visited her folks in California, came down with mono and didn't get back to the city for another couple of weeks. A dozen times while she was gone, Hailey had thought about calling Mac. But it felt so presumptuous, calling him long distance after just one date. He hadn't called looking for her, either. Every time she had talked to the office, she had expected a message from him. But there was none.

"When I got back to town, I finally got up my nerve," she told Pam. "It had been almost two months since our date. I didn't have his home number, so I called him at work. The receptionist said he'd be back from his honeymoon in a couple of days."

"Honeymoon?" Pam sat bolt upright in her chair. "He got married?"

"I figured he was a first-class dog, kissing me like that while he was planning to marry someone else."

"You should have slammed the phone down on him today."

Maybe she should have, Hailey thought. Then she remembered the way Mac had sounded. Sort of tentative, but with a voice as deep and smooth and masculine as she recalled from that long-ago night. She shook her head. "I can't be mad. He loves his wife."

"How do you know?"

"I saw them at a party once," Hailey explained. "It was a few years back. It was one of those big media receptions, the sort of thing Jonathan couldn't stand—''

"Was there any sort of party your ex could stand?''

Hailey ignored Pam's usual Jonathan-bashing. "Mac and this stunning redhead were standing over to the side of the crowd, drinking champagne and laughing. A guy I was talking with knew them and told me she was Mac's wife.'' She sighed, remembering the curious jealousy that had twisted through her. It wasn't because the other woman had Mac, but that the two of them had each other, and she and Jonathan had been falling apart.

"Do you think he's still married?''

Looking up, Hailey blinked in surprise. "I don't know.''

"If so, why the lunch invitation? Maybe the man's a dog after all.''

"I don't think so. This lunch is probably what we initially thought. Something to do with business.''

"He said it was personal.''

Sitting up, Hailey frowned. "He did, didn't he?''

"My guess is he's not married, and he's suddenly remembered that one date.'' Pam nodded in satisfaction. "This is good. Your divorce has been final for nearly a year. Jonathan and the boys have been back with his first wife longer than that. You're long overdue for someone to ease you back into the world. Nothing like an old flame for that.''

"How do you know these things?'' Hailey asked her friend, amazed as always by the working of the woman's mind.

"I've read *Cosmopolitan* since I was thirteen. I understand relationships."

With a sigh, Hailey got up and went to her desk. "We have work to do, Pam."

"Yes, we do." The brunette stood and walked slowly toward the desk, rubbing her chin as she studied Hailey. "By Wednesday, we've got to perk you up."

"What?"

"Your haircut's great. But you need some blond highlights. Maybe a new lipstick color. Definitely a new outfit."

Groaning, Hailey lowered her face to her hands. She knew, without a doubt, that Pam would drive her insane unless she followed her advice.

And so on Wednesday, with her hair blonder and her lipstick rosier, wearing a new, soft pink sweater set with a short, pleated gray skirt, Hailey stepped out of a taxi in front of the café where she had agreed to meet Mac. Her morning meeting had run long. She was late and feeling frazzled, her head buzzing with the advice Pam had given her.

Be cool. Even a little chilly. At least until you find out if he's still married and if this lunch is business or pleasure.

Squaring her shoulders, Hailey ducked under a canopy at the top of stairs that led down to a below-street-level eatery. Designed to resemble a New Orleans style café, the restaurant featured outdoor dining on a small, bricked-floor patio near the bottom of the steps.

"Hailey?"

She whirled around and found Mac walking down the sidewalk, grinning at her. Like a million other men in this city, he wore a noncommittally dark suit, standard white shirt and a red-striped power tie. His sandy hair was darker than she remembered, the crinkles at the corners of his hazel eyes deeper, the set of his shoulders broader. But she would have known him anywhere. Just looking at him made her feel as if she were twenty-two and standing in the cold outside her apartment building. All of the advice Pam had given her about being cool fled.

Holding out both her hands, Hailey laughed and said, "Mac, it's so good to see you."

2

Hailey's laughter was just as full and warm as Mac remembered, but she was sleeker, more sophisticated than the woman who had first fascinated him eight years ago. Her face had lost the roundness of youth, leaving behind features of more sculpted symmetry. Beneath the umbrella that shaded their outdoor table from the midday sun, her eyes shone as deep and velvety brown as they had on the cold night when they'd last met. Those eyes were no longer open windows to her soul. Age had brought an inevitable guardedness. Yet the trace of vulnerability he glimpsed beneath her smooth exterior only enhanced her loveliness and added a layer of mystique.

Mac couldn't relay any of these observations to her, of course. Waxing allegorical to a woman had never been his strong suit. He settled for a rather mundane "I like your hair," as soon as the waiter had taken their orders.

Hailey looked uncertain. "My hair?"

"It used to be long."

"Oh." Seemingly relieved, she settled back in her chair. "Thanks. I cut it years ago."

"I guess a lot of things have changed. You're a partner at the firm now."

"That's right." A proud smile curved her lips.

He grinned back. "You told me you'd make it big."

"There are people who attribute my rise to the fact that my father's college roommate's brother hired me. Tom is the Jenkins in the firm's name."

"But you worked your way up."

"Absolutely. Tom doesn't give free rides. My associate, Pam Witherspoon—"

"The woman I spoke with?"

Hailey nodded. "Tom promoted Pam and me to full partner last year. We're handling the bulk of the business now."

Her ambition and confidence were obvious. "You're planning to expand, aren't you?"

"We have some plans," she replied. Wariness crept into her expression. "Is that what this lunch is about?"

Confused, Mac paused with his water glass midway to his lips. "Pardon me?"

"Are you looking to move into PR or something?"

He laughed. Softly at first. Then louder, until he broke into out-and-out guffaws that drew the attention of the other diners sharing the tiny, open-air dining area.

Hailey looked puzzled. "What did I say?"

Mac got a handle on his amusement. "I'm sorry. It's just that the thought of me in public relations is too funny. The work requires tact, so I'd never make it."

She chuckled. "You do have a reputation for speaking your mind."

"So you've heard about me, huh?"

"Over the years, I've even heard you called difficult. Not that I believed it, of course."

"See? You're so tactful. That's why you're a success in your field."

"I guess it was crazy to imagine you were thinking of changing careers. You're making plenty of waves with Day Varner."

"Do you listen to Day's show?"

"On occasion. Your boss's left-leaning views stand out among all the conservatives out there."

"Day and I have similar perspectives on a lot of issues."

"Is Day's politics what took you into radio? As I recall, you were bound and determined to end up producing one of the network's morning talk shows."

"I changed my mind," Mac said, shrugging. "I saw that with radio I had the chance to stretch a little. Television's become so structured. The costs are so high that ratings are all anyone cares to discuss. No one can afford to take a chance."

"The talk show you were working on when we met was taking a few chances. Don't they still mainly feature cross-dressing Nazi kleptomaniacs who hate their mothers?"

Her description of the typical TV talk show guest was on target enough to make Mac laugh again.

"It's true," she added as he continued to chuckle. "The last time I was home during the day, I kept flipping from channel to channel, trying in vain to find something that wasn't about a dysfunctional family whose members had tried to kill one another.''

''That kind of stuff is exactly why I got out of that racket.'' Mac leaned forward, warming to one of his favorite subjects. ''After leaving the show where we met, I moved up to associate producer at another, but it was all so trashy. It wasn't leading where I wanted to go, and I was more and more frustrated. Maybe this sounds trite, but I like to think what I'm doing now makes more of a contribution. Anyone can just fill the airwaves with noise. Day is attempting to be thought-provoking.''

''One could argue that the TV talk shows provoke a certain kind of thought.''

''But I like doing a show without the sleaze, and without simply doing one celebrity interview after another. Some mornings, it seems to me that the network shows are all just one long promotion for someone's new movie.''

''Well, no one can say your show doesn't take on tough subjects.''

''Mainly, I like to throw opponents into the arena and let 'em mix it up with Day as referee.''

''Sounds explosive.''

''Not if you stay on top of things. I guess that's where I got my reputation for being difficult.'' Mac paused as the waiter appeared with their salads.

When the server was gone, Hailey assured Mac, ''I wouldn't say you have a bad rep. Some other PR people I know who have booked clients on your show have simply come away with some definite respect for your...forcefulness.''

"Your tact is showing again."

"You're misunderstanding me. I said they *respect* you."

Mac accepted the compliment, because winning respect as opposed to popularity was his goal. As he explained to Hailey, it was the product that went on the air that was most important to him. "I try hard to get along with the people I'm working with day in and out, but I can't let a guest or anyone from the outside walk in and take over. If they do..." With a rueful sigh, Mac caught himself before he could deliver a soliloquy on one of his favorite topics. "I'm sorry. I tend to get wound up talking about my work."

She brushed off the apology with an airy gesture. "It's okay. I honestly don't know how to react to people who don't care about what they do."

She looked so pretty, sitting forward with her eyes sparkling, her expression full of lively interest. Watching her, Mac's pulse quickened, his senses sharpened as his entire body responded to her natural charm. Perhaps she felt similar stirrings. Her smile warmed, intensified.

Suddenly as nervous as he had been before, Mac cast about for what to say next. His search proved futile, and maybe that showed his friends were right about his needing to get out more.

Hailey seemed not to notice his tongue-tied state. "I suppose it's a miracle that we haven't run into each other in all these years. Our fields tend to intersect."

"I suppose."

She was silent, her eyes downcast as she toyed with the remains of her salad.

Mac shifted in his seat, knowing this was the opening he needed to explain why he had never gotten in touch. "I'm sorry I never called you, Hailey."

She looked up, her expression carefully controlled. "I was the one who was supposed to call when I got back from that author tour."

"Did you?"

Hesitating for only half a beat, she reached for her iced tea. "More importantly—what made you call me after all these years?"

He explained that he had moved and found her name and address in his desk. "I started thinking . . . I wonder what happened to her."

She smiled. "Well, now you know."

There was a challenge in her words, a deliberate now-what-are-you-going-to-do edge to her voice. Mac was considering how he might respond when the waiter reappeared with their entrées. He decided the best course of action would be to pivot. "Tell me more about what you've been doing with your life."

She squeezed a lemon wedge over her plate of grilled chicken and asparagus. "My work is very demanding. It doesn't leave a lot of time for anything else."

"I suppose you've moved?"

"To the Upper East Side."

"My, my," he drawled. "Your fortunes have improved."

"Well, my address is a little farther north than fashionable. What about you? You said you moved."

"I'm across the Park from you. It's an older building that's just been remodeled. I like the big rooms."

"So your fortunes aren't suffering, either."

"My bank account is going to suffer every month when I write the mortgage check."

"You ever think of moving out of the city?"

Mac shook his head emphatically. "Do you?"

"No way." She cocked her head to the side. "Although sometimes I dream about a little house somewhere in the country. Just for weekends."

She had hit upon one of Mac's fondest wishes. "That I could go for. Something simple."

"But comfortable. Rustic, but with the comforts of home."

"With a little stream running through the property. Maybe a garden off to the side. I wouldn't mind growing some vegetables."

"You were raised on a farm, weren't you?"

He nodded, pleased that she had remembered. "In Indiana. My aunt and uncle and a couple of cousins are still there."

"But you and a friend of yours moved here right after college." She recalled more than Mac had expected. "Greg's a cartoonist, isn't he? Has he created his own mega-successful, crime-fighting character yet?"

"He's waiting for his particular hero to be discovered while he makes a marginal living animating the adventures of others."

"I guess it could be worse."

"When he hits it big, he'll make millions off the parents who have to buy every action figure and every accessory that's marketed with them."

Hailey laughed as if she knew exactly what Mac meant. "Including something like a super-colossal, giant, plastic Castle of Doom, which you have to spend half of Christmas Eve putting together."

"Because Santa would never just put out the box and let Mommy or Daddy take care of it in the morning."

She looked appalled. "Of course not. That would be almost as bad as forgetting to eat the cookies left on the Santa plate beside the tree."

"That's the deadly sin, isn't it?"

"No, the deadly sin is waiting until the week before Christmas to go looking for the Castle of Doom and having to drive to Hackensack to find it in a toy store where all the clerks are suffering from severe holiday season battle trauma."

"I've been to that store."

"You couldn't have," Hailey retorted. "This place is straight out of one of Freddy Krueger's nightmares. If I thought that place really existed, I'd start screaming and never stop."

Laughing, Mac turned his attention back to his last bite of Cajun-spiced shrimp. "God, the lengths we go to for our kids." The silence that greeted him made him glance back at Hailey.

She was very still, a butter knife poised over the roll she had plucked from the breadbasket. She looked . . .

stricken was the only word he could find to describe her expression.

"I'm sorry," Mac said. "I guess I'm assuming you have kids."

Her features smoothed out, effectively masking the pain he had glimpsed. "I don't."

Yet she talked like a parent who had lived through the pitfalls and perils of Christmas. Mac wasn't insensitive enough to push for an explanation, though he was puzzled.

"Stepkids," she supplied smoothly.

A surprising pang of disappointment echoed through Mac as his gaze fell to her left hand. No ring was in evidence.

She explained that missing article with a cryptic, "My ex-husband's boys."

He was amazed by his relief. "So you're divorced."

"Nearly a year."

Mac nodded, empathizing with the lack of emotion in her voice. After Eve was gone, he'd found showing pain or bitterness much harder than presenting a stoic face. He knew some people had been put off by his apparent emotionless manner. It seemed oddly important to let Hailey know he understood where she was coming from. "Being alone isn't easy."

"Sometimes the alternative is less endurable."

She'd been badly hurt. Mac could hear it in her voice, though he imagined she'd be chagrined if she knew how the rancor showed. He had to wonder what kind of jerk she'd been married to. He was debating the wisdom of probing a bit when his attention was claimed by a commotion behind them. He turned just in time to see a red-haired streak of lightning dart down the café steps.

"Daddy!" Julianna called, dodging a waiter with a loaded tray as she ran through the crowded outdoor dining area to get to his side.

Mac was instantly up, catching his daughter in his arms just a few feet from his table. "What are you doing here?"

She garbled something about school being let out, but most of the explanation was lost in her hiccups and the tears streaming down her face. Mac couldn't imagine how she had wound up here alone.

A haughty maître d' materialized at their side. "Is there a problem?"

"She's just upset," Mac said, sending apologetic smiles to the diners nearby as he put Julianna down and placed a comforting hand on her small shoulder.

"She belongs to you?" the maître d' asked.

"I'm her father."

"And you are going?"

Mac's smile died. "In a minute."

The man was drawing himself up, apparently ready to protest, when over his shoulder Mac spied a red-faced Sylvia coming down the stairs. His intrepid assistant hustled through the restaurant.

"Julianna," she gasped, dropping to the sniffling child's level to give her a hug. "You scared me to death, running off like that."

Julianna clung to Mac's hand. "I wanted Daddy."

Mac looked quizzically at Sylvia.

She rose to face him. "Her school closed because half the kids and most of the teachers have come down with this violent strain of stomach flu. They decided to send everyone home to try and contain the spread. Evidently this stuff is as contagious as the plague and almost as gross. Nausea, fever, vomiting—"

A woman at the table next to them made a choking sound. Mac murmured an apology and pulled Sylvia and his daughter back toward the stairs and away from the other diners, a move that seemed to please the maître d'. "How did you get Julianna?" Mac asked Sylvia.

"The school called, and I had an errand to run up that way, so I went to get her. You know I've picked her up a hundred times."

"Did you call her usual sick-day sitter?"

"Yes, but she and her kids already have this flu. I figured I'd just bring Julianna to the office and you could take her home after you got back from lunch."

"So how did she get here?"

"We were walking past and she saw you."

"Mean old Sylvia wouldn't let me come say hi," Julianna put in. "So I ran away from her."

"You looked busy," Sylvia told Mac, jerking her head in a crazy way.

He frowned at her. "What?"

"You and your companion." Again, Sylvia made a motion with her head that was a cross between a twitch and tick.

"My comp—" As quickly as he had forgotten her, Mac remembered Hailey and wheeled around. A waiter was hovering near the table he had vacated, so he couldn't see Hailey. "Damn," he muttered, and tried to give Julianna's hand to Sylvia, but the child wailed a protest. Mac recognized the signs of a gathering storm. Lately his daughter had been resorting to tantrums when her usual charm wasn't successful at getting her way.

"Stop it," he said sternly. "You're not a baby anymore, so stop acting like one."

"But I hate Sylvia."

"You love Sylvia. You're just being contrary. Now let me go talk to my friend."

Diners were once again glaring their way, and the maître d' was muttering in a language Mac didn't recognize. Worse, Mac saw Hailey get up from their table and head toward them.

"Please, Julianna, behave for a minute." His child, however, chose to fasten herself to one of his legs while he attempted to smile as Hailey approached.

"It looks like you have a situation," she said smoothly.

"A brat attack," he replied. With as much poise as he could muster under the circumstances, he introduced her to Sylvia and Julianna. The former seized Hailey's hand and pumped it with undue enthusiasm while the latter hid her damp face against his leg.

"Julianna, honey." He took firm hold of her arm and pulled her around in front of him. "Please remember your manners and say hello to Ms. Porter."

His darling daughter, all apple cheeks and long curls and sunshine on most days, simply regarded Hailey with sullen contempt.

"This was nice, Mac, but I should go," Hailey said quickly, sounding as false as her smile looked.

"If you'll wait just a minute, I'll put you in a cab. First let me pay the check—"

Hailey backed toward the stairs. "That's taken care of."

Mac reached for his wallet. "I can't let you—"

"Please don't worry." She started up the stairs, not even bothering to look back as she called, "Goodbye."

Bleakly, Mac stared at her retreating slender legs and trim derriere. He picked his daughter up and, with Sylvia behind him, started after Hailey, hoping to offer at least a more complete explanation and apology. But Hailey was already half a block away, moving along at a rapid clip. Mac didn't blame her for beating such a hasty retreat. When Julianna decided to be a brat, there was a part of him that wanted to run away, as well.

But maybe this was for the best. Maybe fate had sent Julianna past the restaurant today so that a scene would be made and Mac would realize he should stick to his resolve about not dating.

"I'm sorry," Sylvia murmured. "Really, really sorry."

"It wasn't your fault." Setting Julianna down, Mac stroked a hand across her fiery, silky hair. She grinned up at him, her tears gone. Her usual sunny self again, she even hugged Sylvia and apologized.

The three of them started the four-block hike to the office, and were halfway there before Sylvia broke into Mac's thoughts. "Hailey seemed really nice."

"She's just an old friend," he replied, recognizing the inquisitive tone in his assistant and friend's voice. "Don't go reading something into this. I told you Sunday, I'm—"

"Not ready," Sylvia completed.

"Hailey is just someone I knew."

"*Knew?* Then you don't know her now?"

"That's why I called her for lunch. To maybe get reacquainted. We had this date, you see, years ago..." Mac caught himself before he could fall into Sylvia's little trap. "It doesn't matter."

"Because you're not ready." There was something altogether too innocent in Sylvia's tone. He could see she was fighting a smile.

Mac ground his teeth together to keep from giving her more of the details she craved. The rest of the way to the office, however, he could sense her amusement.

At work, Julianna went off to visit with a production assistant who was a friend and sometime babysitter. Mac cleared up a few matters that needed his immediate attention while he tried not to think of Hailey.

Calling her had been just a whim, lunch, a spur-of-the-moment invitation. So what if for just a few, bright moments, she had made him feel like something other than a producer, a father or just a friend? That wasn't solely due to her. He guessed he was coming back to life. The numbness Eve had left with him was finally giving way to normal feelings. His friends had been right to say the move would make him feel like a new man. In the long run, it didn't matter that lunch hadn't gone well with Hailey. They had nothing invested in each other. So why was he feeling so damned disappointed?

Mac gathered up the work he needed to take home with him, stopped at Sylvia's desk and gave her instructions on a dozen different concerns. Feigning serious indifference, he added, "You think it would be a good idea to send her flowers?"

Sylvia, God bless her, didn't ask who "her" was. "I'll do it for you."

"Something small. But nice." He tossed a piece of paper with Hailey's name and address on the desk.

"I'll take care of it."

"Be tasteful," Mac cautioned again, before going in search of his daughter. "Small but tasteful."

"Oh, absolutely."

Four dozen red roses, complete with baby's breath and greenery in a large and elaborate crystal vase, were delivered to Hailey's office just before five o'clock. The arrangement was so huge, so astounding, that receptionist Dolores and bookkeeper Rita, who usually hit the door just as the workday ended, stuck around to see how Hailey would react when she saw it.

"It's so huge that it works somehow," Pam was saying just as Hailey came into the reception area.

Hailey halted several feet from the gargantuan creation. "My God, who died?"

A titter ran through the office staff, but they headed out for the day, leaving only Pam and Hailey to contemplate the flowers.

Pam plucked a white card from somewhere deep in the foliage. "Shall I open this for you?"

"I don't think I want to know who would send this."

The brunette hadn't waited for Hailey's permission to read the card. "It's from him."

Hailey grabbed it and read out loud, "'With my deepest apologies and the hope that we can meet again. Love, Mac.'"

"What exactly happened between the two of you?" Pam demanded.

"I told you we met, it wasn't pleasant, and I'm not seeing him again." That was all Hailey was telling her friend, who had driven her crazy asking for details all afternoon. Hailey wasn't about to discuss the way she had felt when that little red-haired imp had come racing across the restaurant calling for her father. She wasn't about to explore with Pam the pain caused by just the thought of getting involved with another man who had children.

Pam wasn't pushing for details. Instead she was studying the flowers with a thoughtful expression. "He can't be all bad, Hailey. This...mass of flowers here is too much, of course, but you have to admire a man with enough confidence to say things in a big way."

"There must have been a mix-up at the florist. This isn't Mac's style."

Sending her a sharp glance, Pam said, "So you learned enough about him to be able to recognize his style?"

"His style is obvious," Hailey retorted. "He's a busy professional and father. Busy men just call up the florist. And florists sometimes gets orders crossed."

"He's a father? Is he still married, as well?"

Hailey ignored the naked inquiry in her partner's gaze. "Just shut up and help me move this thing into my office. If we leave it here, no one will be able to see Dolores tomorrow. With something to hide behind, she'll never do any work."

It did indeed take two of them to move the flowers. One to pilot, the other to steer blindly behind the hedge-high bouquet. They wrestled it into place on a corner table in Hailey's office, losing only two blooms in the process.

Breathing heavily after the exertion, Pam flopped into the desk chair. "Can you imagine what this cost him?"

"All the more reason to assume it's a mistake."

"Then you should call him."

"Don't be ridiculous. I'll call the florist tomorrow."

"But if he meant to send a small, restrained token of his esteem, isn't that more of a reason to call and give him a second chance?"

Hailey purposefully gathered up her laptop computer, her purse and briefcase. "I'm going home, Pam. Tomorrow, I hope you come up with something new to obsess over. Because, as of right now, the subject of Mac Williams is closed. I'm just not interested in seeing him again."

Pam's smile betrayed her skepticism.

Well-founded skepticism, Hailey acknowledged to herself at home. She struggled through the evening news. She turned to the work she had brought home, but couldn't concentrate on that, either. Finally, she gave in and thought of Mac.

Most particularly, she thought of the way his face had changed when he had seen his little girl today. Blind love, they called it. Hailey understood the emotion very well. She also understood what it was like to stand in a place crowded with disapproving adults while you attempted to placate a stubborn, willful child.

Smiling, Hailey had to give Mac some points. He'd handled today's situation much better than Jonathan would have. Her ex-husband would have simply hustled the child out the door as quickly as possible. Mac had at least tried to soothe his daughter. He hadn't let the snooty maître d' or the other diners keep him from comforting Julianna.

Julianna. The name fit her, Hailey thought. It was as old-fashioned as her cascade of long, loose curls. She had her daddy's hazel eyes. If the redhead Hailey had seen Mac with several years ago was her mother, then that explained her hair color and probably the sprinkling of freckles across her cheeks. Even cranky, she was the sort of little girl you wanted to hug.

Where was Julianna's mother? Hailey wondered. Out of the picture, obviously. Mac didn't act like an attached man, although the child had looked at Hailey with the proprietorial he's-my-daddy-so-you-leave-him-alone look in her eyes that Hailey remembered all too well. Hailey snuggled down in the corner of her couch and recalled the first time she had met Jonathan's boys. Suspicion had warred with hostility in those days with Trevor and Luke. At first she had despaired of winning them over. But when she had...

With a sigh, she closed the door on those memories. The boys were gone. Forever. And that still hurt. A bone-deep ache that had only begun to ease in recent months. Which was exactly the reason why she was wise to steer clear of Mac and his redheaded angel. She had been smart to run away today.

Of course, Mac didn't know why she had fled. He probably thought she was incredibly rude, that she'd been embarrassed by Julianna's little scene. Perhaps she should call, attempt some sort of explanation for her abrupt departure. He was a nice man. She owed him...

Nothing.

Hailey told herself to think clearly. Even without the child, Mac wasn't for her. She still wasn't ready for any man. The wounds from her failed marriage were still too fresh. No matter what Pam said, Hailey knew she needed to stay out of romantic entanglements for the foreseeable future.

"No men. No kids. Just me." Hailey was repeating that like a mantra when her phone rang and she grabbed it up.

"I called him for you," Pam said without preamble.

Unfortunately, Hailey knew exactly who the woman was referring to. "Tell me you're joking."

"I caught his assistant at his office right after you left today. What a delightful, helpful person she is. If we ever get rid of Dolores, we should call—"

"Pam!" Hailey barked. "Cut to the chase."

"She gave me Mac Williams's number at home and now you're meeting him for drinks in half an hour. At the little wine bar down on the corner."

"What?" A glance at the clock showed that would be nine o'clock.

"I told him you were tied up with an important client," Pam continued smoothly. "And that you asked me to call and thank him for the flowers and invite him for a drink. He said yes. He sounds so nice, Hailey."

"Then you go meet him."

"Now stop that. I've known you long enough to be able to tell when a man appeals to you. No matter what happened at lunch today, or what you said, I know this guy interests you."

"Nothing could be further from the truth."

"Don't be that way," Pam wheedled.

"I'm not meeting him."

"That would be rude, considering that he's asking some friend of his to baby-sit and everything."

"I'll call and cancel. I'll tell him you're a psychopathic liar who is posing as a friend."

"I am your friend," Pam said. "That's why I did this. You can't let what happened with the boys and Jonathan sour you on romance. There's a world waiting out there. You've just got to get out there again. The best way is through a transition romance."

"That's terrific advice, Pam. You ought to take it yourself. You head down to the little wine bar and meet the fabulous Mr. Williams. I hope you love him and he loves you, and I'll toss rice at your wedding."

"You know I'm never getting married again."

"I'm going to call him right now and cancel," Hailey said.

Pam sighed heavily. "Okay, Hailey. Call him. If you can get his home number, of course."

"Give it—" The phone clicked and was buzzing in Hailey's ear before she could get the demand out. A desperate search through the phone book and a call to the operator proved that MacKenzie Williams's home phone number was unlisted. An answering machine clicked on at the studio of Day Varner. And Pam wasn't answering, either.

Cursing her, Hailey dropped down on the couch and watched the hands of her mantel clock creep toward nine. She wasn't going. Mac could just sit there for a while and stew. Or better yet, she'd call the bar and leave him a message. And then he'd never bother her again.

She remained motionless on the couch, however, counting off the minutes until it was five till the hour.

Then she sprang into action, stuffing her T-shirt into her jeans, pushing her feet into loafers and grabbing up a tweed blazer and her purse.

All she was going to do was go down there, tell him Pam was nuts, and make her apologies.

She'd be home in fifteen minutes flat.

3

He remembered that she loved champagne.

All thoughts of a rapid departure fled when Hailey approached the table Mac had chosen in the quiet corner bar. A waitress was just setting down two tapered flutes, each filled with a bubbly, golden liquid.

Smiling, Mac stood. "I hope champagne is still your favorite."

She nodded mutely and slid onto a tall chair beside his. He looked different tonight. Maybe it was the jeans and cotton button-down, but he seemed more like the young man in a hurry she had met eight years ago.

He sat, too. "Do you remember telling me that given a choice, you'd take champagne over food?"

Hailey recovered her poise along with her voice. "How can you recall so vividly something that I said nearly a decade ago?"

"The same way you remembered that I grew up on a farm and moved to the city with my best friend."

"I don't know why I remembered that, either."

"Maybe because our one date was particularly memorable."

That made her laugh.

"What's so funny?" Mac demanded.

"Just that if it was so memorable, why did it take us all this time to see each other again?"

"Fate got in the way, I suppose."

She sat back, picking up her glass by its fragile stem. "I don't believe in fate."

"You used to."

"Now that's something I *don't* remember." Hailey sipped her drink. The champagne was crisp, dry and sparkling, exactly as she loved it. She hadn't intended to have a drink, but since he had already ordered, she couldn't let this go to waste. One drink, then she would make her apologies and go.

Mac was studying her with an odd expression.

"What?"

"Eight years ago, you claimed all the major events in your life had happened as if by destiny. You said fate ruled your life."

"I was young and starry-eyed."

"You're still young. Where are the stars?"

"All gone." Leaning one elbow on the table, she rested her chin against her palm and opened her eyes wide. "See? Now, my vision is clear and completely down-to-earth."

"I liked the stars."

The deepening note in Mac's voice took Hailey by surprise. It seemed to her that their gazes locked for just a beat too long. Then he seemed startled, as well. Suddenly edgy, she looked away.

He cleared his throat. "I was really sorry our lunch was cut short today."

"It was no big deal. Thank you for the flowers. They were . . . impressive."

A frown creased Mac's forehead. "That's what your associate—"

"Helpful Pam," Hailey murmured dryly before taking another sip.

"She seems very nice."

"Oh, yes, and very...enterprising." Subterfuge just wasn't in her nature, so Hailey knew she might as well confess what Pam had done. Mac would probably be nauseated by such juvenile behavior, and that would be that.

But after she told him, he laughed.

Hailey stared. "Doesn't that sort of manipulation make you furious?"

He shook his head. "It sounds like something my friends would do to me. If Pam hadn't called my assistant, I'm sure Sylvia or one of the others would have found a way to get in touch with you."

"Why?"

"Because they're bound and determined that I 'get back out there in the dating world.' "

"Oh, God," Hailey moaned in sympathy. "You've got people after you, too?"

"None of them think I can handle my own social life."

"Or lack of a social life."

"Bingo." He chuckled again. "Why is it so wrong to want to be alone for a while?"

"It's not wrong. After a relationship ends, a person needs to get back in touch with themselves. They can't get tied up with someone else right away."

Mac nodded. "That's very true. When you're part of a couple for a long time, that couple becomes an entity of its own. And when one half is gone..." His sigh was forlorn as he picked up his glass again. Then he looked at her. "I'm sorry, Hailey, I didn't mean to get into this."

Quite naturally, she touched her hand to his in sympathy. "It's okay. I understand."

His gaze was intense. "I think you really do."

Removing her hand, she settled back in her seat once more. "I'm going to confess something that makes my friend Pam furious. I haven't dated much since my divorce. I've actually been enjoying being alone." At least part of that was true. She hadn't been lonely for Jonathan. Only the boys.

"But I would imagine there are guys waiting in line."

"Oh, please." Chuckling, she pushed her hair back from her face. "No one waits in line for anyone else these days, Mac. Everyone's just as cautious as we are."

"Kind of sad, huh?"

"Maybe."

Silent for a moment, he drained his glass. "So, tell me, if you're so cautious, why are you here?"

"I told you. Pam called and—"

"You still didn't have to come."

"I didn't want you sitting here waiting. That seemed needlessly rude, especially after you sent me flowers. It wasn't your fault that Pam called you up with a fictitious invitation."

"But you didn't have to stay."

She shifted uneasily in her seat, but kept her retort light. "I never waste champagne."

"In all these years, this is the first time plying a woman with alcohol has ever served me well." He signaled for the waitress. "I'll order another."

His boyish grin relaxed Hailey once again. She knew she should protest and stick to her resolution about leaving. But she didn't. Soon, she had another glass of champagne in front of her. They slipped easily into conversation, just as they had years ago. Mac made her laugh with stories about some of the impossible-to-please guests who had been on the show. Hailey reciprocated with her own clients-from-hell tales.

After they finished their second drink, Mac suggested they go for a walk. Only as they stood to go did Hailey look at her watch and realize her intended fifteen minutes had stretched into nearly an hour.

What was she doing? This man, an intriguing mixture of cockiness and reserve, was not for her. Hadn't she just decided she was too emotionally raw to even think of dating anyone? She should stop this right now.

"It's getting late," she said once they were outside the bar. "I'm sure Julianna—"

"She was asleep before I left," Mac replied. "My friend Greg had come over before Pam called, and he said he'd stay as long as needed."

"How nice."

"If Julianna wakes up, she'll be thrilled. She likes Greg better than me. He gives her all the ice cream she can eat, lets her watch scary stuff on TV and doesn't make her clean up after herself. After he's through with her, I sometimes feel like an ogre."

"Don't worry too much. It looked to me today as if she's pretty fond of you."

Mac turned right, walking toward Fifth Avenue. To hang back would be rude. Besides, Hailey told herself, this was just a walk. No big deal. And it was a wonderful night to be out. The fall air was warm, more like late May than early October. The New York streets were as crowded at 10:00 p.m. as any other city street at noon, but instead of the frantic daytime pace, everyone was strolling, enjoying the unseasonably mild weather.

"About today," Mac began when they had walked a few moments. "I'm sorry my daughter caused such a ruckus."

"I told you it was no big deal."

"But when you left—"

"I needed to get back to the office, and it looked as if you had your hands full. I thought perhaps Julianna was upset because she saw you with me."

"She just wanted her way."

"Pretty typical for kids that age. Is she six?"

"Five." Hastily he added, "And a quarter."

"Oh, my, so she's measuring her age out that way."
Hailey shook her head. "I remember before Trevor
turned six, he counted out the months, weeks and
days. Every morning, we had to figure it out. Was he
five years, seven months and four days? Or was it five
days?" She laughed. "He was so intent on getting
older, and I just wanted him to stay a baby."

"Trevor is your stepson?"

"Yes."

"And he lived with you and your ex?"

Too late she realized they were treading into personal territory she didn't want to explore. "Yes," she
replied, then changed the subject. "Didn't you say at
lunch that you had just moved? How long did it take
you to find what you wanted?"

Mac made small talk about real estate because
Hailey clearly didn't want to talk specifics about her
marriage. That made him even more curious, but in a
way, he supposed it was for the best. She hadn't given
him a personal quiz, either. Julianna had come up,
naturally, but there had been no third degree about
Eve or anything else. He liked that. Hailey made him
feel relaxed, unpressured.

"You know," he ventured when they had been
walking for some time, "this isn't so bad."

"What isn't?"

"Being out with someone."

Her distinctive laugh rolled out. "Are we really *out*
with one another, Mac? Seems to me we were trapped
and made the best of it."

"Maybe that's why it's so much fun. It doesn't feel like a date. Not like one of those let's-get-to-know-one-another quizzes."

"Lucky us. We got that out of the way eight years ago." There was an undercurrent of sarcasm in her tone.

Beneath a street lamp, Mac stopped and turned to face her. "I guess I'm never going to live it down that I didn't call you."

Hailey started to move ahead. "Forget it."

But Mac stepped in front of her again, forcing her to stop. He led her over in front of a lighted boutique window, out of the flow of pedestrian traffic. Earnestly he began, "About what happened back then—"

"You met someone else," she interrupted. "So did I. It's nothing you have to explain to me, Mac."

"But I want you to know—"

"Shh." She silenced him by lifting her fingers to his lips. "You didn't call me, and then you married someone else pretty quickly. It's ancient history, Mac. Forget it."

He realized she must have called him after coming back from her trip eight years ago. She had ducked the question at lunch, but how else would she know he and Eve were married so fast? It was important to him that she not think he had misled her back then.

Taking gentle hold of her wrist, he pulled her hand away from his mouth. "I didn't know Eve when we went out."

She shrugged carelessly, and the movement sent her blond hair swinging forward in gleaming strands. "It was just one of those things. Just a matter of timing. There's no further explanation necessary."

"No, I should have called you. The only excuse I can offer is that I was young and careless and terminally self-involved at that point."

"We were both young," she said, smiling. "And I can't imagine you were ever careless or self-involved."

His fingers were still looped around her wrist, so it seemed quite natural that they slide downward and entwine with hers. Her hand was small, the skin cool and soft. He liked the feel, and she didn't pull away. Instead she looked at him with wide, dark eyes. And she bit her lip. He could remember kissing those lips. After all this time, the sensation came back to him as clear and pleasurable as if it was happening again. In fact, if he swayed a little closer...

Hailey turned her head just before he kissed her, so that his mouth brushed across her cheek instead of her lips. Then she pulled away.

"Mac, I don't want you to think that I'm...that we should..."

"Take up where we left off?" He lifted his free hand to her face, the blunt edge of his finger tracing her strong but completely feminine jaw. "I don't think we could do that, Hailey. We're not the same people we were then."

"Definitely not."

"But I like you still."

She shifted her gaze from his.

He stepped a bit closer. "I think you like me, too. At least you're not running screaming down the street."

A smile crooked the corner of her mouth. "Now, Mac, why would any woman run from you?"

"I've got some pretty intimidating baggage."

"Well, I'm not running," Hailey retorted. "But neither am I suggesting we start dating."

"Why?"

The straightforward question seemed to startle her.

Mac pressed on, "I like you, and you like me. Why shouldn't we see each other?"

"Because I had decided not to see anyone."

"So had I."

"Then—"

"But if we're honest with ourselves, neither one of us really wants that at all."

A frown drew her eyebrows together. "How do you know what I want?"

"If you had no interest in seeing me, you wouldn't be here. Same goes for me in regard to you."

"But I told you—"

"I know, I know, you were tricked by your friend into meeting me," he said, repeating what they had discussed in the bar. "But you're not being honest."

Her frown deepened. "I really resent that."

"Look at me," Mac commanded. "Look me straight in the eye."

She complied, tilting her chin defiantly upward.

"Tell me to go away and leave you alone."

As he suspected, she couldn't do it. Oh, she tried. She opened her mouth, closed it, moistened her lips and attempted to lie. But in the end, she couldn't.

He chuckled in triumph, then kissed her before she could protest. No forethought went into the kiss. No expectations. And yet it was so sweet. So bone-melting good. Damn, but he hadn't expected this feeling.

Hailey moved away. "Mac, we don't—"

He silenced her with another kiss that went on for a good, long while. This time it was Mac who pulled back, and he wondered if his own expression mirrored the dazed look on Hailey's face.

"I think," he whispered, "that both of us could benefit from this."

"You're mighty cocky." She recovered her poise with a saucy toss of her head.

"A kiss like that gives a man reason to be confident."

"You shouldn't put so much stock on purely physical reactions."

"I don't. If I didn't like you, didn't enjoy talking to you, I wouldn't have kissed you. It was more than a physical thing."

She made a soft sound of exasperation. "You're confusing me, Mac. Just an hour ago we were talking about how we each were enjoying being alone, getting used to not being in a relationship. We both admitted to resenting the pressure by our friends to 'get out there.' You seemed as reluctant as I am."

Grinning, he took her hand in his again. "What can I say? An hour with you changed my perspective."

"Oh, don't be silly." Pulling her hand from his grip, she turned to go back the way they had come.

"It's true," he insisted, catching up to her at the corner. "I see now that I've been fooling myself. I am lonely. I do want to spend time with someone."

She made another disgusted sound. "I'm sure there'll be many women who will fill the void."

"Wait a minute." He took hold of her elbow and turned her around. "I'm not talking about filling a void, Hailey."

"Sounded that way to me."

Her meaning took only a second to sink in. "So you think I'm just some horny guy, looking for someone to warm my bed?"

A titter ran through the group of pedestrians gathered around them. Mac sent them an annoyed glance, then pulled Hailey over to the side. "Is that what you think?"

Her expression was carefully blank. "I don't know what to think. Your signals have been mixed all night."

He tightened his hands on her upper arms. "Signals? You sound as if I'm playing some kind of game."

She made no reply.

"I don't play games," Mac continued evenly. "So let me make everything clear. First, I'm still not looking for a relationship. But second, I enjoy being with you as much as I did eight years ago. So, third, I've realized I would really like to see you again."

She opened her mouth to protest, but Mac cut her off with an upraised hand. "And now fourth, I am a normal, heterosexual adult male, and I wouldn't mind following that kiss with several dozen others and maybe something more. But I'm not banking on that. Getting you or anyone else in bed is certainly not my sole intent. My technique may be a little rusty, but back in my bachelor days I never resorted to trickery or games or signals. *Scoring* was never my object or my style."

Hailey let out a deep breath. "Are you through?"

Unable to read her expression, Mac stepped back and shoved his hands into his jeans' pockets. "I guess so."

"Then let me make everything clear to you." Her gaze focused on a point over his shoulder. "I'm a little shell-shocked when it comes to men. I haven't been divorced that long, and like you, I don't want a relationship. At the same time, you're right, I am lonely." Her expression softened. "And I do like you. A lot."

Such simple words shouldn't cause such a surge of exhilaration, Mac thought. But they did.

"I'm sorry I've acted so silly," Hailey continued, looking him in the eye again. "My only excuse is that I'm a little rusty at all of this, too."

"Maybe we should practice on each other."

"What do you mean?"

"Would it be so hard just to see each other again?"

"Just?"

"We get together, see how we feel, take it one date at a time."

"Just be casual about it all?"

"And have a good time." Mac grinned. "At the very least, our going out would probably get our friends off our backs."

She was slow to agree. "I'd just hate Pam thinking she was right about all of this."

"Believe me, I'm not looking forward to Sylvia's smug little smile tomorrow, either. But it sure beats being fixed up with her poodle lady cousin."

Hailey looked confused.

"It's a long story," Mac said. "Maybe I could tell you about it on Saturday night."

"Saturday?"

"I make a really special pasta with sun-dried tomato sauce."

"Sounds impressive. I don't remember you saying you cooked."

"Having a kid keeps you home, and since I like good food, I learned my way around the kitchen."

"I guess your daughter likes that."

"She's into peanut butter and jelly, and she won't be home Saturday night."

Something resembling relief passed over Hailey's face.

"You could bring some wine," Mac coaxed. "We could talk, maybe listen to some music..."

And maybe get in a whole lot of trouble. That disquieting thought made a brief appearance in Hailey's brain. It was replaced by a much louder, *So what?* She was attracted to this man, as he was to her. They each had no interest in long-term commitments, but they enjoyed each other's company. And he was keeping his daughter out of the mix. He admitted to wanting many of the things she had been missing—companionship, conversation, camaraderie. If sex entered the picture, well . . . Hailey was a big girl. She knew how to protect herself. She especially knew how to guard her heart. There was no reason to think she couldn't keep a handle on this situation.

"All right," she heard herself saying.

"Great." His smile was smug, as if he'd known she would acquiesce.

"You're entirely too sure of yourself, Mr. Mac Williams."

"Think so?"

"Absolutely." She let her smile take the sting out of the word, however. Putting out her hand, she headed toward the curb. "I really don't like arrogant men, but if you'd like, you can walk me home."

His fingers closed over hers again, his grin matching hers. "I'd like that very much."

They strolled to her apartment that way—hand in hand. Neither of them said much, but that was fine with Hailey. She was much too busy being aware of Mac to keep up a running flow of small talk. She prided herself on her independence, but she could also admit it was nice to walk down the crowded street with a man close at her side. She liked the warmth of his broad hand around hers. She felt a small but distinct thrill when his arm brushed hers. She savored the deep timbre of his voice. And when they got to her building, she kissed him good-night before he could even make a move.

"Don't look so surprised," Hailey teased as she stepped back.

"Is that how I look?"

"Sure."

"Funny, I'd have thought I looked dazzled." There was nothing bantering about his tone.

Hailey's laughter died. "Mac, don't do that."

"What?"

"Don't go all serious on me. Remember, you said we'd have fun, be casual."

"And we will," he promised. "I'm a little rusty at that, too, I guess. Since Eve died—"

"Eve?" Hailey repeated blankly.

"My wife."

As the words sunk in, a dull roar started in Hailey's brain. "Your wife died," she said, knowing she sounded dim-witted.

Mac nodded. "Early last year."

"You never said."

"I'm sorry. I suppose I assumed—"

"I assumed you were divorced."

"Well…" He shifted awkwardly from foot to foot. "I'm not." Frowning, he added, "Is there something wrong, Hailey? You seem—"

"I'm just surprised." She struggled to get a grip on her whirling mix of emotions. "We didn't discuss this."

"It didn't come up," Mac said. "Should it have?"

He looked so distressed that she couldn't say anything. She certainly couldn't tell him that his wife being dead made a lot of difference, that it changed everything.

Hailey conjured a smile. "Don't mind me," she said with an airy wave of her hand. "I'm so tired I'm not making sense."

"Then I'll see you Saturday night." He gave the address. "About seven?"

She nodded, he said a last good-night, then waited until she was safely inside the building. When she waved goodbye, she hoped he couldn't see how stricken she was.

His wife had died.

That terrifying knowledge sent Hailey straight to bed.

Mac floated home. Or so it seemed. The walk felt as if it took only half as long as it should have. He knew he was crazy to let an evening with this woman go to his head, but he couldn't stop himself, either. When he opened the door to his new condo, which seemed like home in a way it hadn't until now, he was whistling.

And in a scene that seemed eerily familiar, Greg was waiting not far inside the door. But unlike the days when the two old friends were roommates, Greg was holding Mac's daughter in his lap.

Mac, smelling trouble, let his whistle die.

"I hope you had a good time," Greg said.

"Why?"

"Because you've got big problems here."

As if on cue, Julianna held out her arms for her dad and began to cry.

4

—●◄—

"I don't get it. What does it matter if his wife died or divorced him?"

Pam's question made Hailey cringe. Not because she didn't expect it, but because her companion's voice rang out so loudly in the hushed environs of the Metropolitan Museum of Art's Astor Court Chinese Garden. Reproduced as a Ming Dynasty scholar's courtyard, the serene surroundings were designed for quiet thought and minimal conversation. Hailey should have known better than to bring up the subject of Mac here.

"So he's a widower," Pam continued. "Why are you so upset?"

"Please," Hailey pleaded as other Saturday afternoon museum browsers sent annoyed glances their way. "Not so loud."

Pam managed to stage whisper, "I'm sorry. My voice naturally rises when I'm stupefied over something you've said."

In response, Hailey tugged her to the exhibit exit and in search of an area more conducive to the conversation she had been trying to avoid. The other woman knew Hailey was going to dinner at Mac's place, that he wanted them to get to know each other, to have some fun together. Pam had gloated about that. She also knew Hailey was nervous. Just after lunch today, she had stopped by, saw that Hailey was bouncing off the apartment walls and suggested this outing to the museum, one of Hailey's favorite haunts, in an effort to distract her before she was supposed to meet Mac. But until now, Hailey had led Pam to believe her nerves were due more to excitement than trepidation. Now Hailey wished she had kept her fears about Mac to herself.

The late Saturday afternoon museum crowds forced Hailey and Pam to keep moving until they reached the first floor. In another courtyard they found an empty seat across from an original Tiffany stained-glass window.

Pam threw herself down on the bench. "What is all this nonsense about Mac's wife?"

"Like I told you," Hailey explained. "She's dead."

"That's terrible. What happened?"

"I don't know, but she was young and beautiful. She had a husband who loved her and an adorable child."

"It's sad."

"It's more than that."

"And it makes you feel..." Pam pursed her perfectly lined and tinted lips, looking confused. "What? Other than sympathy?"

"Don't you get it?" Hailey demanded. "Mac lost his wife tragically, and now he's beginning to venture out in the world again—"

"Sounds like you two are a matched pair," Pam interjected dryly.

"You can't compare me to him. I lost a husband, yes—"

"And two children you loved."

"But they're all still very much alive. It's not the same thing."

A diabolical smile curved Pam's lips. "Yes, unfortunately Jonathan is alive, isn't he?"

Hailey ignored the jab against her ex. "I think Mac has dealt with grief and pain such as you and I can't imagine."

"I see that. What I can't see is why that has you in such a tizzy."

Exasperated, Hailey said, "Sometimes I don't know why we're friends."

Pam sighed and, as if talking to a child, said, "It's because I keep you from sliding into complete dementia, my dear."

"No, you don't. You're the one who drives me insane. And if you don't want to hear this..." Standing, Hailey started to walk away.

"All right, all right." Pam caught Hailey's arm. "Sit down here and explain it to me. I'll try to understand what's got your panties in a wad."

Hailey gave serious thought to running away, but she knew Pam would bug her to death until she explained. And anyway, talking with her friend would keep her from thinking about time creeping inexorably toward the hour when she was supposed to be at Mac's.

"He's in a vulnerable place," she said, sinking down on the bench again. "He's just starting to date after losing his wife early last year. Almost two years have gone by, Pam. That's a long time to wait. That shows how deeply he felt, how hard this is for him."

"So maybe he's been smart enough to wait until he's ready."

Hailey brushed that suggestion aside with a wave. "He's not ready, not by a long shot. He got all sad-looking when we were talking about relationships at the bar. At that point, I was thinking, Yeah, it's tough to divorce, especially with a child involved. I could identify with his feelings. But then, later, when I knew she was dead . . ." She combed her hair back from her face with her fingers.

"Stop that," Pam ordered, taking hold of her hand. "Your hair looks great today, and you're going to ruin it."

Jerking away, Hailey said, "Who cares about my hair? I'm talking about this needy, yearning man. I don't want to get involved with someone like that."

"Then why are you going to dinner with him?"

"He asked before I knew the situation."

"So?" Pam shrugged. "I still don't know why you're so hyper over this. Hailey, you're going to have pasta with the man. Do you really think this will lead to a marriage proposal tonight?"

"Stop being so flip."

"Then stop with the anxiety attacks. If you ask me, he's the one who has the right idea. Didn't you say he wanted to keep things light and casual and fun?"

"That's what he said, yes—"

"So believe him."

"But this isn't a light and casual sort of man. Mac has an intense personality."

With slow, deliberate movements, Pam crossed her legs encased in neatly pleated slacks that matched her blouse. She was just as methodical and careful with her next statement. "You are amazing. You go out with the guy once, years ago. This week you see him twice for a total of what...three hours, maybe? And you already know his personality inside and out."

Defensively, Hailey replied, "He's not hard to figure out."

"Oh, get real." Pam patted the hands Hailey was wringing in her lap. "Go over there, try to have a nice time, try not to project into the future. Just enjoy the moment, the evening. For once in your life, don't borrow trouble."

"But he just reminds me so much of Jonathan."

Pam snorted in indelicate derision. "Mac doesn't sound anything like Jonathan. If Jonathan were in Mac's situation, he would have started dating the afternoon of his wife's funeral."

"That's not what I mean. The men aren't alike, but the situation is. I know you hated Jonathan, but when I met him, he was newly divorced, all alone with the boys, struggling with the after-effects of a nasty divorce. He was in as much pain as someone who had lost a spouse to death, and he wasn't ready for another relationship.''

"And his poor, poor me routine roped you in right away, didn't it?''

Hailey wouldn't exactly classify Jonathan's situation when they met as a routine, but Pam was right about her falling for him. He and the boys had been human equivalents of all the lost and wounded animals she had rescued as a child. If there was one thing Hailey understood about herself, it was her compulsion to try to fix problems.

Pam knew that compulsion, too. "Jonathan used you, Hailey. You got him through a difficult time with his boys, then he up and left you and took them back to England.''

Disinclined to rehash the painful details of her marriage's failure, Hailey didn't comment. "Whatever caused Jonathan and I to get together, it was a mistake. But I could make the same sort of mistake again with Mac.''

"Based on what?''

"Based on the fact that he's exactly the sort of man I swore I wouldn't date ever again. A needy, hurting male who'll take and take and claim my heart and then probably move on. That's why I need to call him and cancel tonight. I should have done it days ago.''

"Would you listen to yourself?'' Pam asked, her impatience showing. "You say Mac isn't like Jonathan, so why should it follow that this situation will turn out anything like your dealings with your ex?''

Hailey fell silent. She hated to admit when Pam started making sense.

Dropping her habitual wisecracking tone, Pam regarded Hailey with sincere concern. "Jonathan hurt you badly. But that doesn't mean every man will."

Because she had never thought of herself as someone who generalized about people, Hailey admitted her friend was right. "I'm just being neurotic, aren't I?"

Not quite answering the question, Pam said, "I think you're really attracted to Mac, and those emotions have you on the run. You don't want to care again, because you don't want to hurt again. And all of that is perfectly normal."

"Then what should I do?"

"You should stay aware of the fact that neither of you wants more than a casual relationship."

Hailey cocked her head to the side. "Of course, you're right."

"I mean, honestly, Hailey, isn't it time for you to take a chance, to stop running? Haven't you paid penance enough for what happened with Jonathan?"

"Is that what I've been doing?"

"Yes, and it has to stop. The first step will be going to Mac's tonight." A mischievous smile flitted across Pam's perfectly made-up features. "Perhaps we can devise a twelve-step program to get you through this. The first step is thinking positively."

Hailey considered the advice for a moment. "I guess you've got a point."

Pam patted her shoulder. "This doesn't have to turn into a big, blown-up love affair. You could just like Mac, enjoy his company, use him to start getting on with your life. You could then part as friends."

"You make it sound simple," Hailey said doubtfully. "If only anything in my life were ever simple."

"You can do it. Just stay in control."

Taking the sort of deep breath most commonly employed by high-platform divers, Hailey said, "All right. I'll try."

"Good girl," Pam approved. "Now all you've got to worry about is being late."

With a frantic look at her watch, Hailey leapt to her feet. She had barely enough time to grab a cab and get over on the West Side to Mac's street, and she still had to buy a bottle of wine for dinner. Unfortunately, half the people in the crowded museum were leaving at the same time. Hailey and Pam were caught in a bottleneck in the building's Great Hall.

"Don't panic," Pam ordered when Hailey began to fret. "I've battled worse than this crowd during the after-Christmas sales." She sprang into action, ducking and weaving, using her elbows as effectively as an NBA center.

In no time at all, she was putting Hailey in a taxi in front of the museum. "Be good," Pam called playfully as the vehicle pulled away. "Freshen your lipstick and make sure you have condoms."

Hailey laughed until she caught the cabdriver's lascivious gaze in the rearview mirror. The confidence brought on by Pam's pep talk fled.

God, what was she doing?

She was still wondering when she pressed the door-bell at Mac's apartment. The urge to run intensified as the door swung open and he stood before her in navy sweatpants and a torn New York Yankees T-shirt. He was unshaven and pale, his hair standing on end.

"Hailey?" he croaked, blinking at her.

A lump formed in her stomach. "It is Saturday, isn't it?"

"Yes, but I called you."

"When?"

"Earlier." He rubbed a hand over his face, as if he were trying to wake up. "I've got the flu. Julianna was sick when I got home the other night. I thought she'd be fine and she could go on her sleepover with a friend. But early this afternoon her friend got sick and then I started feeling bad, and now I'm..." He swallowed, and his skin drained of its little remaining color. "Excuse me." The last words were mumbled as he bolted away from the door.

Hailey hesitated uncertainly on the threshold, then pushed the door the rest of the way open. She took a tentative step into a small, square vestibule with a hallway branching off to the left and a doorway to a kitchen on the right. "Mac?" she called. "Are you okay?"

The sound of a toilet flushing was her only answer.

"I guess you're not." Hailey supposed she should leave, but it went against her nature to desert some-one who was sick. Closing the door behind her, she started to call out again when a moving shadow caught her eye. Around the edge of an arched doorway just down the hall, a small face framed by tangled red hair appeared. "Julianna?" Hailey said.

The head retreated, and Hailey stopped. But in little more than a moment, the girl reappeared. She regarded Hailey with hazel eyes that loomed large in her small, white face. In stretched-out Disney Pocahontas pajamas that sported a large, purplish stain on the front, she looked like one of the street urchins from *Les Miserables*.

In short, she was utterly adorable.

Hailey didn't think before stooping down in front of the child, saying hi and reminding her that they had met. Hailey's gauzy skirt, which Pam had labeled the last decade's fashion mistake, pooled on the floor around her.

Smiling in a way that erased all memory of the tearful and unhappy child Hailey had met at lunch on Wednesday, Julianna said, "I've got a skirt like that."

"I like mine, don't you?"

"It's my favorite, but Daddy says I can't wear it to school 'cause it might make me trip."

Hailey wrinkled her nose. "Dad's are no fun sometimes."

"Yeah."

"Have you been sick?"

The child nodded. "My friend Katie's sick, too, so I didn't get to go to her house."

"I'm sorry. Is there anything I can do to make you feel better?"

"I'm hungry."

As he made his way slowly down the hall, Mac said, "That's a good sign. She's barely eaten since Wednesday night."

Hailey rose, gazing at him in concern. "You look terrible."

He attempted a smile. "Thanks."

"You should get in bed."

"That's where I was when you rang the doorbell."

"I'm sorry."

Waving aside the apology, he said, "I'm sorrier that you walked in on this. I left a message on your machine, postponing our dinner until this plague has passed."

"I've been out all afternoon."

"Well, you should go back out. Run away. As fast as you can. You certainly don't want anywhere near this nasty stuff. Greg was here for only a few hours Wednesday night and he's already at death's door. I can't imagine an outbreak of ebola being this bad."

Hailey shrugged off his concern. "I've always had this incredible resistance to viruses. Must be genetic. My mom's the same way."

"I'm telling you this flu could penetrate a sterile plastic bubble."

"I'll take my chances." With another smile at Julianna, Hailey followed her into the living room and set her purse and the wine she had purchased down on a nearby table. "Mac, why don't I make Julianna some soup while you go back to bed?"

"I can't let you do that. I can handle this." Belying his words, he swayed as he started forward.

Hailey caught one of his arms while Julianna took his other hand.

"You're hot, Daddy," the little girl said.

He was burning up. Alarmed, Hailey ordered him back to bed.

"I will as soon as Julianna gets something to eat."

"I can get her a sandwich or some soup."

In typical masculine style, he was determined to argue. "That's not necessary. I can take care of her." Shaking off their hands, he started forward again, but ended up sitting on the couch. "I'll be okay," he continued to insist. "Just give me a minute, and Julianna and I will be just fine."

Clucking like a mother hen, Hailey helped him to his feet. "Come on, let's get you in bed."

Julianna led the way down the hall to a spartanly appointed and obviously masculine bedroom. Mac continued to protest, weakly, but he also leaned on Hailey and sank down on the unmade bed with a grateful sigh.

"Oh, God," he moaned. "This is what I get for thinking I could invite someone over for dinner."

Julianna, who had crawled onto the bed with him, patted his arm. "You'll be okay, Daddy. I'll look after you."

He smiled, but closed his eyes and leaned back against the pillows instead of answering.

Hailey picked up a large, thermal mug from the bedside table and took it in the bathroom to fill with fresh water. When she got back, Mac muttered something about someone named Phoebe.

"That's my aunt," Julianna explained.

"Call her," Mac mumbled.

Hailey agreed and set the water on the table, cautioning Mac that he needed fluids to keep from dehydrating. His only reply was a groan. She pulled the blinds on the windows and gestured for Julianna to come with her. Half expecting a protest, she was pleasantly surprised when the girl took her hand and walked with her back to the attractively furnished but messy living room.

"Do you know your aunt's phone number?" Hailey asked.

Nodding, Julianna used the telephone in the kitchen, but the aunt didn't answer. Hailey heated some chicken noodle soup in the microwave oven, then shared it and a lively discussion about the Power Rangers with Julianna. They tried the aunt again, still got no answer, but left a message on her machine. Hailey cleaned up the kitchen and tidied the living room with Julianna's able assistance before they checked on Mac, who had to make another stumbling dash for the bathroom. Together, the two females changed the sheets so that he had a fresh, comfortable bed to fall into. He was soon asleep.

A couple of hours later, the aunt still hadn't called. Mac slept on. Julianna, now bathed and wearing a clean, pink-ruffled gown, was curled up on the couch next to Hailey, who was reading her *Sleeping Beauty* for a second time.

When Hailey reached the happily ever after, Julianna sighed. "I just love this story, don't you?"

"You bet."

"Read it again?" To underscore the plea, the little girl slipped her arm through Hailey's and smiled up at her with beguiling charm. "Please."

A warm, familiar glow spread through Hailey. She realized too late it would have been wisest to follow Mac's advice and run away. Not from the flu, however. From this little charmer at her side. She had put herself in peril. Sweet, maternal peril.

But instead of pulling back, Hailey just snuggled closer to Julianna and began to read the classic fairy tale a third time.

Hailey awoke with a jerk and sat up, momentarily disoriented as she stared at the television set across the darkened room. The glow from the screen highlighted a small girl slumbering at the other end of the sofa. Only then did Hailey remember she was at Mac's. If the time on the VCR digital clock was correct, it was almost three in the morning.

Muscles protested as she eased off the couch. Julianna didn't stir, thank goodness. The only time the child had been difficult last night was when Hailey had tried to get her to bed. Determined to stay awake—"In case Daddy needs me"—Julianna had dropped off to sleep about midnight, in the middle of watching a video. Hailey had decided not to risk moving her. She had checked on Mac, who'd seemed to be resting peacefully, and then fallen asleep herself. Yawning, she told herself she should see about Mac again.

A groan filtered down the hall, and Hailey came wide awake as she hurried to Mac's room. In the dim light from the bathroom, she could see him thrashing around on his bed. The sheets were tossed aside, and sometime between now and when she had last looked in on him, he had stripped off his T-shirt and sweatpants. Now he was clad only in boxers that clung low on his hips. His state of near undress made Hailey hesitate for a moment. Then she gave herself a mental shake and went to his side.

She switched on the lamp beside the bed, then took hold of the arm he sent flailing her way. His firm, smooth flesh was damp and burning to her touch. "Mac, it's Hailey. Do you need something?"

His answer was a groan. He pulled away, turned onto his stomach, then instantly rolled over again. His eyes were glazed and feverish as he blinked up at her. "Julianna?"

"It's Hailey, Mac. Julianna's asleep."

"She's sick" was his slurred reply.

"No, she's fine." Instinctively, Hailey put her hand to his forehead. Perspiration had plastered his hair to his head and shone on the rest of his body. Obviously, his fever had spiked, but was hopefully now breaking.

"I'll take care of Julianna," he said, though he closed his eyes.

"You already did."

His only answer was another groan. Hailey went into the bathroom, intent on doing something to make him more comfortable. She found a washcloth in the well-stocked linen cupboard, dampened it and went back to Mac's side.

He sighed when she brushed the cloth over his face and neck. "That feels good."

Sitting on the edge of the bed, Hailey eased the cooling cloth lower, across his broad shoulders and down the well-defined muscles of his chest. He obviously worked out, she thought idly. Hard muscles like these weren't maintained by sitting behind a desk. Her hand followed the fine line of hair that bisected the washboard ridges of his stomach and disappeared under the perilously low-riding waistband of his boxers. Her hand stopped there, though she found herself staring at the masculine bulge beneath the shorts.

Mac sighed, and she snatched her hand away, feeling guilty. He was sick, and here she was, ogling his bod like they were having a picnic at the beach. She was ashamed of herself. But even shame didn't keep her gaze from straying toward that tantalizing bulge yet again. She couldn't help dwelling on the intimacy of her sitting on his bed, of his near-nakedness and her own skimpy attire. Before going to sleep, she had pulled off her long, loose sweater and the black tights that matched it. So now she wore only her gauze skirt and a black, silky camisole.

She really should get dressed, she decided, and started to get up.

"Don't," Mac murmured, his voice thick.

She wasn't sure what he meant, but when she stroked the washcloth over his chest again, he sighed.

"That's good." His eyes fluttered open.

"Feel better?" Hailey asked.

He continued to squint up at her, as if he didn't quite know who she was.

"Go back to sleep," she urged. "You need to rest."

"Yes," he agreed, though he didn't close his eyes.

She eased away, holding up the cloth. "I'm going to dampen this again."

"Drink?" he croaked.

"You want some water? Sure." She helped him sit up, and handed him the mug from the bedside table. He drained it, then lay back against the pillows, looking pale and exhausted.

"I'm going to get you some more ice water," Hailey told him.

She was only gone for a few minutes, long enough to refill the mug and retuck an Afghan around Julianna on the couch. When she got back to Mac's side, he was shaking. Chills had taken over now that his elevated temperature had started to fall.

Hailey straightened out his sheet and blankets and pulled them up and over him. Though he was shivering and saying he was cold, he fought the covers, kicking them aside like a recalcitrant child. Bracing one knee on the bed, she pulled the sheet and blanket firmly up to his chin again. Just as firmly, he shoved them off. His eyes were glassy and wild-looking. Obviously he was half out of his head. But he still needed to be covered.

"Now, listen, bud, I'm not in the mood for a fight." Hailey tugged the covers into place a third time. But

Mac kicked at them again, and she lost her balance on the edge of the bed and fell to his side. The sheet and blanket twisted around her ankles and feet as she struggled to sit up. And immediately, Mac curved his body around hers, one arm and leg pinning her to the mattress.

She pushed against him, but he held on, his strength surprising considering how sick he had been. The only good news in the situation was that he wasn't shaking as he had been. As the warmth from her body transferred to his, he curled tighter around her. She remained motionless until the last of his chills fled.

"Let me go," she then whispered.

He protested and anchored his arm more solidly around her waist. One of his legs snaked in between hers.

"Mac, please let me up."

"Stay with me," he insisted gruffly. "Please."

Just as his daughter's entreaty had led to a third, fourth and a final fifth reading of her favorite fairy tale, his hoarse plea was Hailey's undoing. She stopped struggling and lay beside him, stiff and unyielding and miserable. Minutes that seemed like hours ticked away on the clock beside his bed.

It wasn't that his weight pressing against her side was uncomfortable. It wasn't that she was afraid she was going to catch this flu bug. She was miserable because this felt so perfect. She liked the feel of him against her, all hard and strong and male. She liked the stubble of his beard rubbing her bare shoulder. She even liked the faint but not unpleasant musk of his sweat that surrounded them.

She had to get up, of course. When he woke and became cognizant of what was going on around him, she didn't want to be here, with her skirt hiked up above her thighs and one strap of her camisole trailing down her arm and exposing half her breast. She should get up. She really should. Her eyes grew heavy as she willed herself to move.

Before she could, however, Mac stirred again. The leg he had wedged between hers pressed upward against the juncture of her thighs. Fully awake now, she tried wiggling away, but that only egged him on.

"Mac, stop."

"No."

"But, Mac—" Her words were cut off as his hand slipped from her rib cage up to her breast. His palm moved over the gently peaking mound beneath the delicate silk. Hailey struggled to catch her breath.

"Nice," he murmured, and pushed his thigh upward again.

She edged backward; he resisted. Against her leg she felt the ridge of flesh at his groin grow hard. His thin shorts did little to disguise his stiffening arousal. The bulge that had tantalized her earlier was impressive, indeed.

The minute that thought went through her head, Hailey gasped. What was wrong with her? Assessing Mac's physical attributes like he was a piece of meat wasn't her style. Maybe Pam was right. Maybe she had been spending too much time alone. Regardless of that, right now she had to get out of this bed before this crazy situation got any worse.

With another sigh, Mac's fingers pulled away from her breast and settled high on her stomach. His head fit into the hollow of her shoulder. He snuggled closer, his erection still nestled intimately against her thigh, though his muscles relaxed and his breath dropped into the even cadence of sleep.

She let out a relieved breath. Now she had another chance to get up. Her mind knew what she had to do, but her body seemed curiously reluctant. What was she doing? The longer she stayed, the harder it would be to move. The bed was so comfortable, their positions so very pleasant. Lying here with Mac just felt so right.

Giving in to temptation, Hailey cuddled against him. She stroked his forehead, breathed in his masculine scent, trailed her hand down the muscles of his arm. Heaven, she decided, was being this close to a man like Mac. Even though he didn't even know she was here, she could revel in this moment. It was foolish, and she knew it, but she supposed one more foolish moment where he was concerned wouldn't do any harm.

She closed her eyes, promising herself she would get up in just a moment.

5

---→ ←---

Mac knew he was being watched. The sensation pulled him from the deep reaches of sleep, made him struggle through the yards of cotton that seemed to be wrapped around his head. Cautiously, he opened one eye. Light slanted through the blinds, telling him it was daytime. His daughter was sitting cross-legged near the foot of the bed, regarding him with intense interest. She smiled and he tried to grin back, though his lips were so dry he could barely move them. On his other side, Hailey...

Hailey.

The sight of her snuggled into the rumpled sheets of his bed made Mac sit up. Unfortunately, the hasty movement sent the room spinning and also jostled Hailey awake.

She pushed herself up, blinking, dragging a hand through tangled blond hair. "What is it?"

"Good morning," Julianna said with a sunny smile.

Hailey yawned. "Morn—" The situation must have hit her then, because she let out a squeak of alarm and jerked the sheet up to her chin, hiding the tantalizingly brief black garment she was wearing.

Julianna seemed blithely unaware of anything. "Are you guys ready for breakfast?"

"No...I mean...yes," Mac sputtered. "You go get breakfast for yourself."

"I want Hailey to do it."

"Julianna—"

"I'll do it." Hailey threw off the covers and made a dash for the door, long skirt flying. Seeing that she was almost fully dressed filled Mac with an odd mixture of relief and disappointment.

Julianna took off after her. Mac was left to lower his aching head to his hands to try to remember exactly what had transpired last evening. He recalled getting sick and Hailey showing up for dinner. But the rest was distinctly out of focus. He had a vague memory of being hot and then cold, of someone whispering comforting words, of stroking his face, his chest...

The possibilities presented by such caresses were disturbing, to say the least. Not unpleasant, exactly. In fact, the memory of sensual contentment teased at the edges of his mind. The sensation floated around him like a lingering bit of feminine perfume. What in the hell had happened? He couldn't remember Hailey getting in his bed, but there she had been, beside him. And Julianna had found them that way. God, he couldn't believe this. Since his daughter hadn't seen any women but her mother in Daddy's bed before, she was sure to have some interesting questions.

Tossing aside the covers, he was relieved to find he'd kept part of his clothes on. He conquered his dizziness and made it through a partially reviving shower.

The smell of bacon and coffee wafting from the kitchen turned his stomach, but he managed to pull on jeans and a shirt.

Moments later, in the kitchen doorway, he watched as Hailey lifted a couple of pancakes from the stove's griddle to a plate. Julianna was talking a blue streak, as usual, and didn't see him. Hailey's back was to him, but he could see that she had combed her hair and put a long, black sweater on over her skirt. She was listening with rapt interest to Julianna talk about her friend Katie.

"I always take my teddy bear to Katie's," Julianna said as Hailey set the plate of pancakes and bacon in front of her at the breakfast bar. "Katie's mom lets us have a tea party for the bears with little cakes and biscuits and..." Her forehead wrinkled as she tried to complete the menu.

"Tea?" Hailey suggested.

"Juice." With her spoon, Julianna carved a glob of butter from the tub at her elbow and slathered it on her pancakes. "I like to go to Katie's. She's got a bed with a canopy, and me and her sleep together."

She looked up with an angelic smile. "Just like you and Daddy did last night."

Mac was seized by a fit of coughing. Hailey whirled to face him. For an extra long beat, they just stared at one another. Then Hailey gathered her dignity around her like a mantle. She turned back to his daughter, who was pouring syrup over her pancakes in complete unconcern for what was happening to the adults around her.

"Julianna, honey," Hailey said sweetly, "your Daddy and I didn't really sleep together. He got really sick early this morning when I went in to check on him. I sat with him until he went to sleep, and then I dozed off, too. But I wasn't in there with him all night. You and I spent most of the night on the couch."

"We did?" Again that sunny smile appeared on a mouth rimmed with butter and sticky syrup. "Daddy, did you hear that? Hailey let me sleep on the couch. How come you won't?"

He tore his gaze away from Hailey to answer his daughter. "Because the rules say we're supposed to sleep in our beds."

"Oh, yeah. I forgot to tell Hailey that rule." The child's mischievous look indicated that that omission hadn't been an accident.

"You're a scamp." Hailey reached out to ruffle her hair. Julianna giggled in delight.

Coming to rest against the cabinet across the room from them, Mac said, "It looks to me like you two girls became good friends last night."

"Your daughter is a doll." Hailey's voice was light and impersonal, the same as the glance she sent his way. "Can I get you anything?"

He rubbed a hand across his stomach. "Not just yet."

"You shouldn't have gotten up if you weren't feeling like it. It's no problem for me to stay with Julianna."

"I wanted to talk to you."

She turned and poured herself a cup of coffee.

"About last night," he began.

Hailey ignored him. "Julianna, do you want more pancakes?"

"No, ma'am. Can I be 'scused?"

"Sure."

The child scampered away, and soon the sound of television cartoons trickled in from the living room. The very air in the kitchen seemed to still.

"Julianna likes you. She rarely bothers to excuse herself to me."

Hailey just continued to drink her coffee.

Mac tried again. "About last night...I'm sorry you had to stay. It seems like I remember telling Julianna to call her aunt."

"We left a message, but she hasn't called back."

"So you got stuck here."

"I didn't mind."

"Really?"

"Like I said, she's a dream."

"And what about me?"

She stared down at her mug for moment, biting her lip. Her face was scrubbed clean of makeup, and the fresh, natural look erased some of her sophisticated poise. She seemed young and vulnerable when she finally raised her gaze to meet his.

"I'm very embarrassed," she said.

"Because I was so sick you wound up sitting up with me half the night?"

"I didn't mean to fall asleep in your bed, Mac. But it was late, and I guess I was just so tired I fell asleep. I certainly didn't intend for Julianna to walk in on us."

"I think she bought your explanation."

"I would never want her confused or upset—"

"It's okay," he cut in. "I'll handle it if she has questions."

"I know you will." With a sigh, Hailey set her mug down on the tiled countertop. "If you don't need anything else, I'll take off now."

"You don't have to."

"Oh, but I do."

The firmness of her voice told Mac she was still upset about something. "Hailey, if anyone should be embarrassed, it's me. Here I invite you over, don't cancel until the last minute, then pass out and leave you to play nursemaid to me and baby-sitter to my daughter. This wasn't what I had in mind when I said I wanted the two of us to have fun." He chuckled. "This is certainly not the way I'd want to get you in my bed."

She didn't laugh.

"Sorry," he said, clearing his throat.

She pushed her hair back from her forehead. "I should have known better."

"What does that mean?"

"Just that I've never had much luck with light or casual or easy. I'm just a natural magnet for trouble."

Mac was struck by the sudden certainty that if she walked out now he might not see her again, and he wasn't quite sure why. "What's going on, Hailey? You can't be this upset about falling asleep in my bed."

Shaking her head, she started toward the living room. "I just need to go."

"Hailey, talk to me." He caught her hand as she passed him. He also caught the sweet scent of her perfume. The fragrance brought back instant, sharp memories.

His hand crooking around a breast.

His body pressing against soft curves.

His sex reacting with a hardening, pleasant ache.

One by one, the images clicked into place. This was what he had been trying to remember after he woke up. This was what had happened last night in his bed. This was why Hailey was acting so jumpy. God, what must she be thinking of him?

"I wasn't thinking clearly last night," he said, holding tight to the hand she tried to withdraw from his grip. "I wasn't trying to take advantage of you."

Pink color spread across her cheeks. "So you remember?"

"I think so. I hope I'm remembering everything. I'm really sorry."

"You shouldn't apologize. I had every opportunity to get up and leave you alone. But I didn't."

He blinked. "Excuse me?"

"I should have gotten up." The pink on her cheeks had deepened to red and spread down her neck. Yet she met his gaze straight-on. "I didn't want to."

A pleasant glow began to filter through Mac. "You didn't?"

"But I should have," she insisted. "I don't know what was wrong with me."

He grinned. "If you're worried that I might mind your staying, let me reassure—"

"That's not the point, Mac."

"Explain it to me."

Hailey would much rather run away than attempt any sort of explanation of the confusing impulses and emotions that had kept her in his bed last night, but she suspected Mac wasn't going to let that happen. As she opened her mouth, however, the buzz of the doorbell cut her off.

Almost immediately, a key jangled in the lock and a feminine voice called out, "How's the sick ward?"

Julianna's cries of welcome filled the apartment, and a woman appeared in the doorway to the kitchen. A very beautiful woman. With sleek auburn hair and perfect skin, wearing a hunter green sweater set that Hailey knew Pam would salivate over.

The beauty hesitated for only a second, then a dazzling smile lit her features as her gaze met Hailey's. "Well, well," she drawled, shifting her focus to Mac. "It looks like I shouldn't have worried about you and Julianna."

Mac dropped Hailey's hand faster than if she had stung him. Before she could react or he could say anything, the woman thrust out her hand. "I'm Phoebe Rankin, Mac's sister-in-law."

"Aunt Phoebe?" Hailey said.

"That's right," the woman replied, then swept Hailey toward the table.

The image Hailey had formed last night of a sweet, old, gray-haired aunt in a rocking chair rapidly disin-

tegrated. Not that Phoebe wasn't nice. She was absolutely charming. She was also Mac's late wife's sister.
Which might explain why he fumbled over the reasons why another woman had spent the night with his
daughter and him.

Phoebe, it turned out, didn't give a damn for Mac's
explanations or anything else he had to say, either.
Zeroing in on Hailey, she rattled off several dozen
questions while she pulled bagels and cream cheese
from the bakery bag she had carried in. Hailey, who
was quite frankly dazed by the woman's technique,
answered with equal speed.

Mac sat to the side, looking as uncomfortable as
Hailey felt. Of course, this was awkward for him.
Hailey could understand that. Couldn't Phoebe see he
was embarrassed and on edge? It was bad enough that
Hailey was probably the first woman he had dated in
a long time. But to have Phoebe know Hailey had
spent the night made the situation even more sticky. It
didn't matter that the woman didn't seem to care. Mac
did. And all Hailey wanted to do was get out of here
as quickly as possible.

Finally, Mac brought the interrogation to a crashing halt when Phoebe placed a toasted bagel in front
of him and he shoved it back at her with blatant rude-
ness.

"Well, my goodness," Phoebe said, settling hands
on her slender hips. "What's wrong with you?"

"I told you I didn't want anything to eat," he retorted.

"This bagel will settle your stomach."

"That's a crock."

This was the opening Hailey needed. She stood. "I really have to go." She turned to Phoebe. "I was just leaving when you came in. Now that Mac's up and about, I knew Julianna would be fine."

"Please stay. I'd love to visit with you some more."

"We'll talk some other time," Hailey lied.

Mac remained seated, the picture of gloom, and didn't say anything.

Giving him a nervous smile, Hailey said goodbye and quickly left the kitchen. Passing through the living room, she grabbed her purse and made the appropriate responses to Julianna's entreaties for her to stay. She left the child in front of the television and had just made it to the vestibule when Mac's arm shot around her and held the door closed.

"I'd like to finish our conversation."

She didn't even turn to face him. "I think we have."

She felt him go perfectly still behind her. "I don't get this, Hailey."

"I'm sorry."

"Why are you so upset?"

She said nothing, and slowly he stepped back. She opened the door and left without looking at him. She took the stairs two at a time, berating herself as she gathered speed. Instead of listening to Pam, she should have followed her instincts and stayed far from the third-story home of this compelling, sexy and sweet single dad and his adorable little girl.

Down on the street, Hailey turned east and walked quickly away, just as she should have last night.

* * *

"Gee, thanks," Mac said to Phoebe after he had returned to the kitchen. "I'm sure Hailey enjoyed being put through your personal version of the Spanish Inquisition."

"You're the one who was sitting there doing an imitation of the Grim Reaper."

"I told you I was sick."

Phoebe grinned teasingly. "You looked pretty frisky when I first walked in."

"Then why didn't you leave?"

"Because I wanted to meet her."

Mac rubbed a weary hand over his face. "Just go home, Phoebe."

Taking hold of his arm, the woman led him back to the table and pushed him down in a chair. "I'm sorry. I wasn't trying to chase her away. I liked her on sight, and you know I'm thrilled that you're seeing someone."

"We're not seeing each other."

"So she was a little put off. I'm sure she'll be fine when you call her."

"I don't think she wants me to call."

Phoebe started to protest, then reconsidered when Mac glowered at her. "But why?"

"I guess I'm not her type."

"She seemed just right for you."

"God, Phoebe, don't say things like that. You make it sound like we had a thing going—"

"She was here all night."

"And as I told you, I was unconscious most of the time. Nothing went on here between us." *Nothing much,* he added to himself, and couldn't stop a guilty surge of warmth to his face.

Phoebe's eyes narrowed in suspicion.

"Just stop it," Mac told her, losing his patience. "All Hailey and I wanted to do was get to know each other, but that didn't work out, and I suppose she doesn't want to try again."

"But things will work out next time. There won't be any flu. I can take Julianna. I'll even cater you an intimate little dinner." Stepping back, Phoebe framed the table with her hands while a dreamy look stole over her face. "I've got this wonderful Victorian lace tablecloth. We'll do some flowers, some candles—"

"No."

"She'll love the romance," Phoebe continued, ignoring him. "What woman wouldn't?"

"That woman," he answered. "Because she's not going to see it."

"Mac, I'm trying to help you."

"Then stay out of it. If you're going to plan romantic evenings, do it for yourself."

"Don't be ridiculous." Her movements jerky, she began gathering up the plates of uneaten bagels.

Mac had known her long enough to know something was up, and after what she had just put him through, he thought she was due for some meddling. "Hey, Phoebe, just where were you last night?"

"None of your business."

"But you're like my own sister. I need to know what sort of mischief you're getting into."

"You don't need to know anything," she said, setting the plates in the sink with a clatter that was quite unlike her. "Attend to your own life, Mac Williams."

"That's exactly what I'd like to do, if everyone would leave me alone."

"You should be happy you have such good friends."

"Oh, yes, I'm thrilled." He sighed. "Yesterday, Sylvia confessed that the flowers she sent to Hailey for me cost nearly two hundred dollars. She said she was trying to impress Hailey for me."

Phoebe tsk-tsked. "I wish Sylvia had called me. I could have helped her choose something for half that amount."

"Half? How about for around forty bucks."

"Now, Mac, what can you get for forty dollars?"

"That's not the point," he said, voice rising. "I told Sylvia to send something small and tasteful. But in her haste to *help* me, she went overboard. I don't need her help, or yours, thank you very much, end of discussion."

Phoebe's mouth thinned. "Fine." Several moments of silence passed while she ran water in the sink.

Mac knew it was too good to last.

True to form, Phoebe said, "There is just one piece of advice I'd like to give you about Hailey..."

Groaning, he buried his aching head in his hands.

The door to Hailey's office banged open. Pam stepped inside, clad in a soft and smart scarlet jersey dress that made Hailey feel instantly frumpy. In Pam's waving fist was a pink message slip.

"Problem?" Hailey asked, steeling herself for trouble.

"Why did you tell Dolores to take a message if Mac called?"

"Because I don't want to talk to him."

"That's stupid."

"I beg your pardon," Hailey replied, calmly picking up the pen she had laid to the side.

Pam stalked to her desk and threw the message down. "I might understand if you'd tell me what happened Saturday night."

"I told you he was sick."

"But that's no reason not to talk to him."

Under no circumstances was Hailey going to tell her friend about crawling into bed with Mac. Pam would think it was funny and no doubt talk her into seeing him again. And Hailey was through with that. Mac and his daughter were a danger to her heart and her peace of mind. She wadded the message into a ball and tossed it in the wastepaper basket.

"You're upset over something that happened." Pam's gaze sharpened.

Hailey hated it when her friend looked at her that way. She squirmed in her chair, but didn't reply.

"You're wearing comfort clothes. That's always a signal that you're upset."

"I'm sure I don't know what you mean."

"Yesterday you had on a five-year-old, navy suit with a big, loose jacket."

"So?"

"And today's it's that sweater you've owned since I've known you."

Hailey looked down at her comfortably roomy pink sweater tunic. Though she did feel like a tank in it, she said defensively, "This was an expensive sweater that still looks good."

"It also hides a body bloated by mass quantities of nacho chips and Rocky Road ice cream—which is also what you do when you're upset."

"You're insane."

"And you need to call Mac." Sighing, Pam dropped into the chair in front of the desk. "Lord, Hailey, didn't we talk this out Saturday afternoon? What else do I have to do?"

"Just get over it," she told Pam bluntly. "I'm not seeing him again."

Pam pursed her lips. "You're not helping yourself. What about all the benefits of a transitional relationship? Have you forgotten that?"

"Of course not."

"Then what are you going to do about this?"

"See someone other than Mac," Hailey lied.

It was clear her friend wasn't buying that. "Oh, really? And just who would that be, seeing how you've rejected the advances of every man who has come near you in the last six months?''

But Hailey knew the only way she was going to get Pam off her case about Mac was to substitute someone else. "If you must know..." She paused, searching frantically in her head for another man. "I'm going to call..." Her gaze fell to the paperwork on her desk, where she spied the name of a sports agent with whom they had done some work. "Dennis O'Bannon."

"I thought you said he reminded you of a toad."

"Well, there is that old saying about having to kiss a lot of toads..."

Pam made a gagging sound. "I don't think anyone meant that literally."

"Dennis is a very nice man, and he's asked me out several times," Hailey said. "Believe it or not, I have taken to heart all the advice you've been giving me. I know I should just be dating, playing the field, and that's what I'm going to do."

"All right." A smug smile played across Pam's lips. "If that's the case, then give old Dennis a call right now."

Hailey cleared her throat nervously. She had never really meant to call him. Frantically scanning her desk for an excuse, she said, "I was going to do it later. I'm in the middle of—"

The phone receiver was thrust forward. Hailey looked up into her friend's smug expression. "Call him," Pam challenged. "If you dare."

Trapped, Hailey took the phone and looked up Dennis's number from the letter on her desk. Unfortunately, his secretary put her right through. Worse, he was thrilled that she had called, and invited her to dinner Friday night. There was nothing Hailey could do but make the date.

With a triumphant laugh, Pam swept from the office in a swirl of scarlet jersey, leaving Hailey to simmer in a red haze of annoyance and frustration.

No doubt about it, this woman was a looker. A lush-breasted, slim-hipped brunette who could drive a man less sex-starved than Mac into a frenzy. Sitting on her sofa watching her pour him a glass of wine, he sent a mental thank-you to Greg for arranging this date.

The beauty's name was Krystal. She was just twenty-one, a dancer and aspiring actress. She brimmed over with confidence and sex appeal and even seemed intelligent. So what if she had admitted over dinner that she'd seen the Brady Bunch only in reruns? So what if she'd never owned an actual LP and thought Springsteen's career began with the "Born In The USA" album? She liked Mac well enough to have invited him up to her place for an after-dinner drink. And it was only nine-thirty. He didn't think he was misreading the invitation in her body language.

He'd had some recent experience in interpreting women's signals. In the full two weeks since the disaster with Hailey, he had been pleasing his friends by dating the women they had offered up like so many sacrificial lambs. All dates had fizzled badly until now. But with Krystal, Mac was ready, he thought, more than ready for a night of mindless physical pleasure.

"You've got a great place, Krystal." He glanced around at the ultra-feminine, floral-draped studio apartment.

Smiling, she handed him the glass of wine and settled back against pink sofa cushions. "My mother decorated it."

"Your mother?" Mac echoed, his enthusiasm dimming somewhat. The statement seemed to extend the eleven years that separated the two of them in age.

"She and Daddy worry about me being safe and happy here in the city."

Daddy. Mac had a sudden, intense vision of Julianna speaking exactly this way about him in about fifteen years. The image bit into his libido. He took a long drink of wine. "So your parents support your career aspirations?"

"Actually, Daddy wants me to go to law school and join his firm."

"Really?" Mac tried to keep his expression bland.

Krystal sat up, a movement that sent the skirt of her short black dress climbing up her shapely thigh. "I guess you think I'm not smart enough for law school?"

"I didn't say that."

"I graduated magna cum laude from Columbia."

"That's very impressive."

"I'm not just a great pair of breasts and a tight butt."

Mac almost choked on another swallow of wine. He couldn't remember a woman ever referring to her body in quite this way. But this girl—*woman*—was poised in the extreme. And maybe this was simply how many young women talked these days. He offered a hasty apology. "I wasn't implying that your very...*obvious* beauty meant you couldn't be intelligent."

Krystal must have realized he meant what he said. A smile curved her lips as she took the wineglass from him and scooted closer to his side. "I like you, Mac."

She kissed him before he could reply. It was a pleasant kiss, a very arousing kiss. He had almost relaxed into it when Krystal pulled back, murmuring, "So, you're into monogamy?"

He blinked. "What?"

Seemingly not noticing his discomfiture, Krystal slipped an arm around him. "Greg said you were married, like for forever."

"For six years." That only seemed like forever when he realized that Krystal had been about thirteen when he and Eve got married.

Krystal kissed his neck. "No sideline stuff?"

"Sideline?"

Giggling, she explained, "I mean, did you have affairs?"

The question made him sit up. "No."

She giggled again, and though it wasn't an unpleasant sound, Mac found himself comparing her laughter with Hailey's full-throated chuckle. Then he shook his head to clear the thought. Hailey wasn't interested in him, while Krystal...well, she was kissing him again and asking him how many women he had slept with since his wife had died.

That question made Mac set her away from him. "How many?"

Krystal straightened, her giggle disappearing. "I do have a right to ask," she said. "I mean, God, Mac, a person has to be careful."

Hailey had told Mac the dating world was full of cautious people these days. He understood the need. The days of free and easy couplings had been long past even before his marriage. Lives hung in the balance. Certainly, he didn't want to endanger himself or anyone else. And yet he felt a sadness. There was something about combining a sexual history quiz with foreplay that robbed this moment with Krystal of romance.

And without that crucial element, Mac thought maybe he wasn't ready for a night of mindless pleasure. Moreover, maybe such nights just didn't exist. At least not for him.

"Is there something wrong?" Krystal asked, looking genuinely troubled. "Did I upset you, mentioning your wife? Greg said—"

"You didn't upset me," Mac assured her.

Krystal's expression softened; she snuggled close, reaching for him again.

But Mac held her off. "You are such a beautiful girl, Krystal."

She gazed at him for a moment, then sat up. "Why do I think you're going to brush me off?"

"I'm not," he denied. "It's just that you're right. These days, a person has to be careful."

"I can assure you there's nothing to worry about with me."

He shrugged. "Just because we've got a green light, does that mean we have to speed through it?"

For all her talk of caution, the concept was obviously alien to her. But she didn't reject it outright. In fact, by the time Mac had collected his jacket and she walked him to the door, she had decided to be flattered.

"You're really sweet," she whispered before kissing him soundly once more. "Call me."

Sweet.

The word rolled around, treating Mac's brain like a pinball machine as he headed for home. "Sweet" was the boring equivalent of "good personality." Mac Williams wasn't sweet. No one had ever accused him of such a thing back in his rowdy young stud days. But how else could one describe someone who had just left a young, nubile, not-uninteresting, not-unintelligent woman who had wanted to share her bed with him? With *him,* a man who had been without sex for longer than he would have believed possible just a few years ago. And all because he needed something as elusive, as fleeting, as romance.

There must be something wrong with him, he decided. He used to be able to get his body working just fine with mere paper images of the flesh-and-blood temptress he had just left. And yet that was the worst of this calamity. His body had worked, had responded to Krystal. The landing gear, so to speak, had been in perfect position. It was his mind that had put on the brakes. He was a living, breathing example for all those women who believed men thought with their libidos. He wasn't sure whether to be proud of his newfound sensitivity or worried for his masculinity.

Whatever the case, he was morose by the time he got home and found that Greg, Julianna and Sylvia had turned the living room into one large, blanket-draped maze.

"You're back way too early," his assistant admonished, climbing out from under the afghan that was spread between two wing chairs.

"Must have been bad." Greg popped up from behind the sofa. "Jeez, Mac, how could you blow a date with a girl like Krystal?"

Julianna came crawling through the blankets, demanding, "Didn't you kiss her?"

Hauling his daughter up in his arms, Mac asked, "Who said I would be kissing anybody?"

"Greg."

Mac lifted an eyebrow as he turned to his friend.

But Greg just shrugged. "Hey, man, she asked me a question, and you always tell me to be honest with her."

"So why didn't you kiss her?" Julianna pressed.

Setting her back on her feet, Mac made a lighthearted reply, "That's none of your business, doll-baby."

Sylvia harumphed in disgust. "Oh, great, Mac, that's the way to be open and honest with your kid."

Before he could protest, his daughter made a face. "I'm glad you didn't kiss her, Daddy. I'd rather you kissed Hailey."

Greg said, "Now there's an idea." Sylvia laughed, and Mac just scowled.

Julianna continued, "Hailey was nice. She smelled good and she read to me and made pancakes. I liked her."

"A ringing endorsement if I ever heard one." Sylvia shot Mac a look of triumph and took the little girl by the hand. "Come on, sweetie pie, let your old buddy Sylvia get you ready for bed. Maybe while we're gone your silly old daddy will realize the error of his ways."

Mac watched them leave the room, then ignored Greg while he began gathering up the blankets that were draped over every piece of furniture.

But his old roommate wasn't shy about offering an opinion. "The kid's right. You ought to call this Hailey chick."

"She isn't a chick," Mac objected. "And she doesn't want to talk to me."

"What'd you do to her that night, anyway?"

"Nothing."

Greg chuckled. "Maybe that's what went wrong. Maybe she wanted—"

Mac's glare cut him off.

"All right, all right," Greg said, holding up both hands as if in surrender. "I didn't mean to offend you.

All I'm saying is that you've had a few dates now, you've admitted that you don't want to do this solitary, single-dad thing all the time, but the only woman who seems to interest you is Hailey."

With a mirthless laugh, Mac folded a comforter into a sloppy square. "Maybe the problem is the type of dates I've had. When I kept refusing her cousin, Sylvia set me up with a friend of hers, a performance artist who showed me her pierced navel while we were having lunch."

Greg, of course, looked interested.

"Trust me," Mac said. "It wasn't appealing."

"And what was wrong with that friend of Phoebe's?"

Mac shuddered. "I told you I walked into that metaphysical food store where she works, and before she even said hi she told me my aura needed to be fluffed."

"Maybe you should have let her fluff away," Greg suggested with a comical leer. "Could have been fun."

Grunting, Mac tossed the last of the blankets in a heap on the floor and flung himself down on the sofa.

Greg sat down opposite him. "So what happened tonight?"

Unwilling to admit to his lady-killer friend how he had reacted to Krystal, Mac just shook his head.

"I have two pieces of advice for you," Greg said, sitting forward and lowering his voice. "Call Hailey. Then have some fun."

Mac laughed. "You do like to break things down to their most basic level, don't you?"

"All I know is you had the hots for this chi—I mean, this *woman*, eight years ago. You still do. It's an itch that's begging to be scratched."

Greg's description of his feelings were crude and yet they held a trace of truth Mac wasn't keen to admit. Thankfully, Sylvia chased Julianna into the room before he had to. Hailey wasn't mentioned again before Greg and Sylvia left, and he put his daughter to bed.

But as he pulled her violet-sprigged sheets up around her, his daughter gave her own opinion. "You should call Hailey."

Suspicious, Mac asked, "Did Sylvia or Greg tell you to say that?"

Julianna shook her head. "I just like her, Daddy."

As Sylvia had said, his baby girl's endorsement should be good enough, Mac thought as Julianna snuggled down. Leaving her night-light burning, he flipped off the bedside lamp and went back to the living room. He stared long and hard at the telephone and at the book beside it where he had recorded Hailey's home number two weeks ago.

With a murmured, "What the hell?" he finally called.

She answered on the fifth ring, just as the answering machine clicked on. And she didn't hang up when Mac identified himself.

"Oh, my," she said, sounding almost relieved as she switched the machine off. "I'm so glad you called. Can you hang on?"

He heard some mumbling in the background, the unmistakable rumble of a man's voice. Probably a date, Mac thought, wondering at his jealousy as he listened to footsteps and a door closing. Then Hailey came back on the line. "Mac? I'm sorry—"

"No, I am," he cut in. "I shouldn't have called so late. I didn't mean to interrupt—"

"No, no, I'm glad you did. I mean . . . that is . . . it's no big deal."

Mac fell silent for a moment. "I guess I'm being a pest, calling like this."

"No."

He took another deep breath. "You were upset when you left here a couple of weeks ago. I was sorry about that. That's why I called you at the office. But when you didn't call back, I knew . . . well, I knew I'd blown it."

"It wasn't you," Hailey said quickly. "It was me. I was . . . well, I was just weird."

"Because of me. I'm really sorry." He bit his lip and attempted a small laugh. "It seems like all I've done since we reconnected is apologize to you."

Now she was silent.

"But even so, I was hoping . . ." Mac paused, fumbling for exactly what he wanted to say. He'd had no clear plan in mind when he called. But there was really only one course of action. If his daughter was going to advise him on who he dated, he should include her in the deal. "Julianna and I were hoping you might want to meet us in the park tomorrow."

"Julianna?" Hailey echoed faintly.

"She told me just tonight to call you. She likes you."

"Oh." Another pause stretched between them.

"Hailey?" Mac ventured finally. "You still there?"

"Yeah."

"Well?"

She sighed. The sound was long and wistful and so sad that Mac was expecting her to turn him down.

Instead she said, "What time do you want to meet?"

6

She could blame it on Toad-face. Sitting down on a bench near where she had agreed to meet Mac and Julianna, Hailey told herself this was all Dennis O'Bannon's fault. She had gone out with Toad-face three times in the past two weeks, and if one moment with him had made her stop thinking about Mac Williams, she wouldn't be here now. Indeed, the second and third dates had been just to satisfy Pam's continued challenge.

Last night had been the worst. She and Dennis had just come into her apartment, and he had kissed her—a toady, sloppy kiss—and she had been praying for something other than her right hook to get him out of there. Then Mac had called and saved her.

Hailey figured the answer to her prayers deserved at least a few hours of her time this afternoon. And if she were totally honest, it was more than relief she had felt when she had heard Mac on the phone. She simply liked him. Despite all her reasons for staying away, she wanted to see him again. Maybe, if they called a moratorium on romantic inclinations, they could just be friends. Instead of "practice" dating with one another as they had planned, perhaps they could simply spend time together in a purely platonic, wholly casual way.

It was a good scheme. Unfortunately her brain didn't transmit the details to her body. Because when she saw Mac striding down the park trail toward her, Hailey's heart raced, her palms began to perspire, and all she could think of was how it had felt to lay beside him in his bed. She could feel his smooth skin and hear his deep, slumbery voice. And, God help her, she regretted he had been half out of his mind with fever; she wished he had followed through on his persistent touches and suggestive murmurs.

While she tried to push her disturbing desires aside, Hailey was thankful Julianna presented such a vocal and demanding distraction. Otherwise, Hailey was afraid she might have betrayed to Mac some of what she was feeling. She nevertheless felt light-headed when she was forced to look from the child and into his warm, hazel-eyed gaze.

"You doing okay?" he asked, a slight frown drawing his eyebrows together.

Hailey shook off her silly, weak-at-the-knees feeling and resolved to keep a tight rein on her libidinous thoughts throughout the rest of the afternoon. *Think friendship,* she told herself while assuring Mac that she was just fine. To his daughter, she said, "What do you want to do today, sweetie?"

"We're going on the boats."

"I promised her we'd rent a rowboat," Mac explained to Hailey. "I hope that's okay with you."

"Sure."

With Julianna skipping ahead of them, they set off down a path to the boathouse located near Central Park's midsection.

Mac surprised Hailey by taking her hand. "I have to confess," he said so softly his daughter couldn't hear, "I was more than a little afraid you wouldn't be here today."

"And I have to confess that I thought about not coming."

"Why?"

Hailey looked away. "It's too complicated to explain."

"You could try."

"I'd rather not."

He seemed reluctant to let it go at that. "I've missed you."

Though the words stroked across her with all the power and sweetness of a kiss, she was determined to maintain her equilibrium. So she laughed. "That sounds like the biggest line of all time. Why would you say something so trite?"

"Because it's true."

"You can't miss someone you barely know."

"Do we barely know one another?"

"Of course." Instead of looking at him, she focused her gaze on Julianna's bobbing copper ponytail some five feet in front of them.

"Every time I'm with you, I feel like we've been friends for a long, long time."

Again she chuckled. "Another line. Mac, what am I going to do with you?"

"I have some suggestions."

She started a sassy comeback, then saw the seriousness of his expression. He wasn't kidding around. "Don't," she protested, pulling her hand from his.

"Don't say what I'm feeling?"

"Don't try to sweet talk me."

"I've never been any good at that sort of thing, so I wouldn't try. I'm just being honest. I do feel as if I've known you forever, and I have missed you. It's been a long two weeks."

She was instantly concerned. "Has something happened?"

Now he chuckled. "Let's just say that I've come to see that you are definitely the only woman I'm interested in dating right now."

She studied him in silence for a moment and decided to be truthful, as well. "Unfortunately, you're the only man I want to see."

"Do you have to look so glum about it? What's the problem with me, anyway?"

Hailey drew to a stop. "I've already told you I don't want to talk about this."

"But if we've got this mutual attraction thing going, why can't we discuss it?"

"Because I don't want to," she responded with spirit. "Because it's a perfect day and your daughter just wants to go rowing and so do I. Let's not ruin this by analyzing everything to death."

He fixed her with his steady, all-seeing regard. ''I think you're scared, Hailey Porter.''

She couldn't deny that. ''What if I am?''

Again he grinned. ''Then that makes two of us.''

The statement disarmed her, charmed her. She recognized the melting sensation inside herself. She knew all her well-intentioned resolves about this man were once more thawing like a late spring snow beneath the bright sun. Mac was providing the heat, and she was fighting a losing battle. If she stayed with him today, there would be no running away, no backing off, no excuses. She and Mac would have to see where this ''attraction thing'' was going to lead them. But it helped to know he was as frightened as she was by the possibilities.

Julianna prevented any further personal discussion by racing back to them, demanding, ''What are you doing? The boats are this way.'' She took one of Mac's hands and one of Hailey's. They had little choice but to follow her to the lake where boaters were stroking past.

Mac rented a rowboat and they set off across the water. And there, in the cool October breeze with the flaming leaves of autumn as a backdrop and a little girl's trilling laughter as an accompaniment, Hailey truly let the magic of the day take over. Mac was a tease who kept Julianna giggling, but the girl gave as good as she took, repeating one corny knock-knock joke after another, driving both adults to the brink of insanity. The only way to stop her seemed to be singing. Mac's slightly off-key baritone started the first chorus of "99 Bottles." Julianna joined in, then Hailey. For more than a hour they kept it up, running through the all-time greatest hits of every kid in the U.S., from "B-I-N-G-O" to the completely appropriate "Row, Row, Row."

Back on dry land, they wandered through the park, dodging Sunday afternoon in-line skaters, bicyclers and joggers. In the Sheep Meadow, they joined a crowd gathered around a couple of folk singers. They bought ice cream and held hands and watched kites sailing high in the clear blue sky.

Late in the afternoon in the grass at the meadow's edge, Julianna sat in Hailey's lap, a solid little body snuggled in complete contentment against hers. Julianna was sticky and warm and smelled like milk and modeling clay—a peculiarly pleasant combination Hailey associated with most children her age. When Mac looked at his daughter, there was a tenderness in his expression that made Hailey's chest ache. The pang intensified as he wiped a dried smear of ice cream from Julianna's face with practiced ease and tied her shoestrings for perhaps the tenth time with patient care. And when she went gamboling off, turning somersaults and laughing with uninhibited glee, he looked at Hailey as if she could understand the pride that was bursting out all over him, as if she should share it.

For Hailey, the afternoon was painful in its sweet simplicity. Days like this were what she had shared with Jonathan and the boys in the beginning, what she had missed the most. So, today, with Mac and Julianna, she was like a starving woman, invited for a few hours to a banquet she hadn't attended in years. She knew she'd be sorry later, that she'd suffer for her overindulgence, but she wanted to make sure she didn't miss a single moment of this delicious treat.

She barely hesitated when Mac invited her home for an early dinner. Who could resist his smile? Who could turn down Julianna's "pretty pleases"?

They grilled chicken out on the tiny terrace, and served it with steamed rice and broccoli that Julianna tearfully refused to eat. Mac dealt with her tantrum with firmness threaded with impatience. He wasn't perfect, Hailey saw with something akin to relief. Like any father, he could lose it after a day with a five-year-old.

While Julianna was sent pouting to her room, he and Hailey talked about books, about movies and television and their work, about favorite vacations and childhood pets. She kicked off her shoes and curled up on the couch. He drank a beer as the last light of the day faded. They tidied the kitchen together, and both accepted Julianna's hugs of apology. After her bath, she asked Hailey to read her a story. It was all very domestic, very easy and felt much too natural.

By nine o'clock, Hailey was a dazed puddle of yearning.

Damn it, she didn't know why this all had to feel so good. Why couldn't there be a misstep? Why couldn't Julianna turn ultra-bratty the way kids that age so often did? Why didn't she get tired of talking to Mac? She needed a reason, any reason, to get out of here.

It didn't come.

Later, hovering in Julianna's bedroom doorway while Mac pulled the covers up to his daughter's chin, she heard the child whisper, "I think you ought to kiss Hailey, Daddy. Just like Uncle Greg said you might kiss that other lady."

Hailey didn't stick around to hear Mac's response. She wasn't even concerned about who that "other lady" might be. She adjourned to the living room, where her stomach knotted and she twisted her hands together. The very air in the apartment was filled with expectation, a feeling even the cool breeze from the open window couldn't dispel. To calm herself, she wandered around the room.

It was a pleasant space, with shining hardwood floors, colorful rugs and a sofa and chairs covered in nubby fabrics of deep green and rust. Pottery lamps glowed on low oak tables. On the walls hung several paintings filled with life and energy. The large street scene on the wall opposite the window held Hailey's interest the longest. The painted figures seemed to actually be in motion. She could almost hear the murmur of voices and the roar of traffic. She studied the painting for a long time before noting the artist's signature.

At the same moment the name sunk in, Mac spoke from somewhere behind her. "It's Eve's."

Nodding, Hailey said nothing.

"She had a flair for capturing movement."

Hailey contemplated the painting for a moment more before turning slowly around. "What happened to her, Mac?"

His voice was even as he looped his thumbs in the pockets of his jeans and walked toward Hailey. "She had this backache. It didn't go away. We thought it was from toting Julianna around. When she finally checked it out with the doctor, he did tests. She had an ovarian tumor. It was malignant, and the disease spread fast."

Try though she did, Hailey couldn't stop her soft cry of distress.

"It was difficult to grasp at first," he continued in the same impersonal sort of tone. "Maybe because it was so fast. But then, that was Eve's way. She never did anything slow."

Hailey stepped closer to him, instinctively offering comfort. "I can't imagine how you coped with it all. Especially with Julianna. She was so young."

"Julianna was my rock." For the first time his voice wavered. "If I hadn't had her..." He cleared his throat. "Well, if not for my little girl, I think I might have wanted to die myself."

Hailey slipped her hand through the crook of his arm. "I'm sorry, Mac. I didn't mean to pry or bring up sad memories."

"There's no reason why you shouldn't ask about Eve."

"You loved her very much."

He drew in a deep breath, released it just as slowly. "Yes, I did. But she's gone."

"But still—"

"No," he said, suddenly taking both her hands in his. "Don't think I'm still mourning her, Hailey. I'm not. I'll always miss her, but she's gone and I'm still here. And it's only been in the last couple of weeks that I've realized there are more reasons than just my daughter for me to be glad I'm alive."

Hailey didn't want to hear that she might be one of those reasons. He might think it was true, but it couldn't be. As she had said earlier today, they still barely knew one another. It was too soon for either of them to be making rash statements or big plans.

"You look scared again." Mac threaded his fingers through hers.

"That's because I am."

"I don't understand why. The same as I'm not sure why I'm so scared."

"Neither do I."

He chuckled. "What a pair we are."

"That's what scares me the most—that we could even think of ourselves as a pair."

"But it's happening that way. We've both resisted, but it's happening anyway."

She stepped into his arms. Not because she thought she should. But because there was nowhere else she *could* be at this moment. To stay separated was simply impossible. They fit together well, her chin resting on his broad shoulder, his arms encircling her without awkwardness or hesitation. He pulled her tight against him. Every nerve ending in her body felt alive, aware, awaiting his caress.

"I really want you," Mac murmured, his voice husky.

The words were unnecessary, since she could feel the tightening of his body where their hips met. Hailey simply nodded, not trusting herself to say anything.

"I've always wanted you. From the minute I saw you across that studio eight years ago, I wanted to feel you." His fingers slipped up under her loose cotton sweater and came to rest against the bare skin just above the waistband of her jeans.

She arched her neck as he kissed the sensitive spot beneath her ear. He murmured, "I wanted to taste you."

Twining her arms around his neck, she lifted her mouth to his. The kiss was at once new and yet familiar. She expected the surge of want, but the intensity was shocking. She knew Mac experienced the same body-rocking wave of need, for his kiss deepened. His hands dropped to cup her bottom, and he lifted her up, urging her legs around his hips. They melded together, torso to torso. The sleek muscles of his shoulders and back knotted and strained beneath her hands. Yet he didn't break their kiss as he carried her down the hall and into his room, where the bedside light provided fittingly romantic illumination.

He placed her on the edge of the bed, then pulled away with one last kiss before closing and locking the door. The sound of the lock's click told Hailey there was no going back. And why would she want to? Facing Mac in this dimly lit room seemed as inevitable and as right as any act of her life. She had claimed to no longer believe in fate. But this was preordained. Nothing this perfect could be anything other than destiny.

With her gaze fastened steadily on his, Hailey grasped the hem of her sweater and lifted it over her head.

Mac stepped forward and took the garment. He brought it to his face, breathing in the scent of her, the sweet aroma that had teased his memory the morning they had awakened together, the same fragrance that had lingered on his sheets for days.

Smiling, he said, "You're looking less and less scared by the moment, Miss Porter."

She grinned back, then reached up and unsnapped his faded, worn jeans. Gaze locked with his, she pulled the zipper down and cupped his hardened, aching sex through the thin fabric of his shorts. The caress made him sigh, then groan. Stilling her hand, he pulled her up and into his arms again. He thought he could go on kissing her all night. Kiss her for the sake of kissing alone, without the expectation of anything more. She tasted just right, moved just right, felt just right.

But tonight wouldn't end with a kiss. Hailey's hands were on his body, guiding his knit polo off, tugging at his jeans. She whispered sweet words of encouragement in between kisses that grew more and more heated. She didn't pause until he had kicked his jeans and shorts aside and stood naked in front of her. Then she sat back on the edge of the bed, arms braced behind her as she looked at him, at the erection that grew almost painfully rigid under her gaze.

A smile, pure as an angel's and yet suggestive as an imp's, teased the corners of her mouth. "Oh, my," she whispered. "My, my."

He said nothing, but the approval and anticipation in her expression was as arousing as her touch. He pulled her to him once more. Her jeans quickly went the way of his. Small breasts, tipped by tightly budded pink nipples, swayed forward when released from her lacy white bra. Panties, mere scraps of silk and lace, skimmed down slender legs.

Mac stepped back, taking pleasure in her slim but soft curves, in her gently rounded belly, in the nest of golden curls that guarded her feminine mound. "Worth waiting for," he murmured. "Definitely worth waiting eight years for."

Her laughter was full and rich, as uninhibited as she looked standing naked beside his bed. "We should have thrown caution to the wind eight years ago. Before gravity started taking its toll."

"Gravity?" Grinning, he drew his thumb down the valley between her breasts, then cupped each firm orb in his palms. "Seems to me gravity has been nothing but kind."

Laughter turned to sighs while he stroked her breasts. Sighs became murmurs of pleasure when he eased her back on the bed and his tongue took over the arousing motion of his fingers. He tasted and teased, lingering over her deliciously responsive nipples until she parted her legs and brought his hand to the moist, warm folds of her sex. She guided him without shame to the sensitive kernel hidden there. He circled it once, twice, a third time. Hailey's hips arched upward, while his name escaped her lips like a prayer.

Her pleasure made Mac throb. He was heavy with need, almost desperate for release. Hating to leave her but knowing he must, he murmured a quick, "Stay just as you are."

When he returned from the bathroom with a box of small foil-wrapped squares, Hailey sat up and took it from him. Putting the condom on became a sexy game, a kiss-and-touch-and-tease affair, far easier than the awkward, clinical moment he had feared. Smoother still was the way he slipped between her legs and inside her hot, lush depths. They found a rhythm right away, merging their bodies, blending their mutual passion with a grace that felt innate, effortless. They moved together like long-time lovers who had choreographed this scene before, who knew how to match their steps and build their desire.

Mac had to wonder at the freedom he felt. Mostly, he just wanted the dance to last. But it had been a long time for him, and the sensations he was feeling were just too intense to sustain. His climax came quickly. "I'm sorry," he whispered as the first swell of release cut through him.

Hailey shushed him with a kiss. She wrapped her legs tighter around his straining hips, welcoming him with an open, direct abandon.

But when it was over, when minutes had passed and he could breathe again, Mac slipped to her side and looked at her in regret.

She answered his unspoken apology with a kiss. A long, tender kiss filled with all the reassurance any man could need. But if that weren't enough to convince him, there was also her hand moving down his body and the luminous glow in her brown eyes when she pulled away.

"You okay?" he asked.

"Perfect."

"I wish—"

She cut him off with another kiss. "There's not one thing I would change about tonight, Mac. Not one thing I would change about the whole day."

Completely content, he pulled her close. "Does this feel as natural to you as it does to me?"

"Too natural. I'm getting scared again."

"Don't think about it." He claimed her lips, then murmured, "There are other things to think about."

"Like what?"

He pressed his hand between her thighs, one finger sliding into the slick cleft and eliciting a soft sound of pleasure from her.

"There's that," Mac told her before bending forward to taste the perspiration that beaded in the hollow of her throat. His finger probed deeper, seeking again her most private, pleasure-intensifying button of flesh.

Sighing her approval, Hailey closed her eyes and let her thighs fall farther apart.

"And there's this." One finger was joined by another as he found the spot he sought.

She stretched like a cat, and arched her hips against his circling fingers. Turning her head toward him, she looked into his eyes and smiled, a sleepy, dazed smile. Their gazes remained joined as her breath caught, as her body bowed upward and she trembled from the force of her orgasm. Reaching down, she stilled his fingers, but held him tight against her pulsing heat.

Watching and feeling her climax was perhaps the most erotic moment Mac could remember experiencing. Had there been other moments like this for him? They faded from memory as he reveled in the sheer sensuality of the present, in the unbridled sexuality of the woman he held.

When her pleasure had peaked and passed, she smiled at him again. "That was nice. Very nice. But now I'm more frightened than ever."

He tucked a wayward strand of her blond hair behind her ear. "Go to sleep."

"I can't stay here."

"Why not?"

"Julianna."

"She's already seen us in bed together."

Hailey peeked down at their naked sprawl of limbs. "This is different."

"This is good. But we could put on something and get under the covers."

"She might still be confused."

"She'd get over it."

"Mac..."

Groaning, he admitted she was right, that hitting Julianna with a lover in his bed—even a lover she seemed to adore—might not be the smartest move. But neither of them made a move to get up and dress.

"I'm so tired," Hailey said around a giant-size yawn.

He lifted her hand to his lips. "And happy, I hope."

Hailey was afraid to admit the joy she was feeling. Because it was too strong, too complete. It had to be wrong, she told herself. This runaway train they were on was surely going to jump the tracks. Anything that had happened this fast couldn't be trusted.

She started to express some of her worries to Mac. But he had fallen into a sudden, dead-to-the-world slumber. Opening her mouth to protest, Hailey smiled instead. Tenderly. Then fearfully.

God, she had done it now. She had gone and fallen in love with this man. In love with him, with his daughter, with a scenario she craved to be part of.

Hadn't she known this would happen?

Hadn't she told Pam?

Hadn't she promised to guard her heart?

She was in trouble. Deep, deep trouble.

Hailey was ready to run again until she looked at Mac. At the thick fan of his eyelashes. At the stubble of his beard. At his tousled sandy hair, strong arms and muscular chest.

She remembered laughing with him over dinner. She recalled the tender way he held his child. She relived, in excruciatingly gratifying detail, the way he had stroked and filled her body.

The truth was, she didn't want to run.

So if he broke her heart, as she fully expected, she'd have no one to blame but herself.

Foolishly perhaps, she shunted that thought aside and lay watching him sleep instead of leaving as she knew she should.

And it wasn't heartbreak that was on her mind when she slipped down his body and brought him completely awake by taking him into her mouth.

She had thrown off her doubts by the time he finally put her in a taxi outside his building at 3:00 a.m.

And she was feeling utterly satisfied, not worried, when she made it into the office a full hour late.

Pam, who was standing at the reception desk when Hailey came in, peered at her with sharp, all-seeing eyes. The other woman's eyebrows arched in approval as she surveyed Hailey's trim black suit with blood-red piping. It was her favorite suit, her I'm-sexy-and-I-know-it outfit.

"Oh, goodness," Pam purred. "Someone's feeling very good this morning. Someone had a wonderful weekend."

Hailey picked up her messages and sailed past her friend and down the hall to her office.

Like a bloodhound on the scent of a fox, Pam followed and closed the door behind them. "There's just one thing I want to know. Tell me it wasn't Dennis O'Bannon who put that smile on your face. I don't want to think that I misjudged that man so badly."

"No," Hailey replied with a giggle she couldn't suppress. "I've given up Toad-face for good." She paused. "I traded the toad for a prince. For Mac."

Abandoning all pretense at sophistication, Pam did a jig around the desk while chanting, "Yes, yes, yes!"

7

$\longrightarrow \bullet \longleftarrow$

"Julianna, stop squirming, please."

For what seemed like the hundredth time in the past ten minutes, Mac tried to complete his daughter's Halloween costume by tying a black cape around her wiggling form.

"It's hot," she complained.

"Then don't wear it."

"But then I won't look like Catwoman. You're the Joker, and me and Hailey are Catwomen." She stuck out her lower lip and folded her arms across her chest, staring in disapproval at her reflection in the full-length mirror on his bathroom door.

"You have to make up your mind," Mac told her. "It's either wear the cape and be hot or leave it here."

"I want to be Catwoman," was her irrational, teary reply.

Mac counted silently to ten. "Julianna…" The buzz of the doorbell put a halt to his lecture. "That must be Hailey," he murmured, and walked out into the hall. He wanted to get the door before Greg or Phoebe, who had dropped by unexpectedly and were in the living room, could.

Julianna ran to her room, shrieking, "Nobody can see me until I'm Catwoman. Nobody."

Choosing to ignore her histrionics, Mac met Phoebe near the doorway. She demanded, "What's wrong?"

"Don't ask."

The doorbell pealed again. More screams of dismay erupted from Julianna's room. Phoebe started forward, but Mac caught her elbow. "Leave her be. She can't keep throwing these tantrums in order to get attention."

"But it's Halloween," Phoebe protested. "She's just overly excited about the party at Katie's."

"She's overly bratty, too."

Greg, who had joined them, looked alarmed. "Aren't either of you going to do something about her?"

"No," Mac retorted, and again strode toward the door. "I'm not. And neither are either of you." He swung the door open, and a smile quickly replaced his frown. Idiotic grins were becoming a habit when Hailey was around. And she was around a lot. In the week and four days since they had become lovers, she had spent every spare moment with him and Julianna.

She looked particularly fetching tonight. Her costume was a grown-up version of Julianna's. A sleek black leotard and tights encased her slim curves. Tied over her shoulders and swirling around her black-booted feet was a black cape lined with purple satin. A black mask covered the upper half of her face. Whiskers had been drawn on her cheeks. To complete the look, a perky set of black ears peeked out of her blond hair.

"I've come for you." Her chuckle was deep and sultry and ended on a purr as she stepped forward, whispering a suggestive, "Would you come for me?"

Forgetting about the audience that the open door had hidden from Hailey's view, Mac accepted her kiss, let it deepen. Only when he heard choked laughter and a clearing throat did he remember his sister-in-law and best friend. Breaking the kiss, he took Hailey's arm, pulled her inside and closed the door.

She stood staring at Phoebe and Greg, a tide of crimson streaking up the part of her face not hidden by the mask.

Feeling oddly protective, Mac gripped her hand. "Look who's here. The real Catwoman."

Phoebe reacted with the sort of aplomb Mac might have expected. Hand outstretched, she said, "You look wonderful, Hailey. I can't wait to see you and Julianna together."

Hailey took her hand, but still said nothing. Mac filled the awkward silence with an introduction to Greg, who was his usual affable and flirtatious self. Hailey recovered her poise and managed to say hello before Julianna's anguished wails issued forth once more.

"What in the world?" Hailey asked.

"We have a cape crisis," Mac explained.

"Well, for goodness' sake." Moving past the other adults, Hailey went down the hall and knocked on

Julianna's door. "It's Hailey, honey. I want you to see my costume."

"Go 'way," came the tearful reply.

"But I thought we were going to be twins."

"I hate my costume."

"But since it's just like mine, maybe I can help."

There was silence, then the patter of footsteps, then the door creaked open and Julianna's head appeared. "All right. You can come in." Hailey went inside and the door shut everyone else out.

"Well, well," Phoebe murmured. "It would seem that the new girlfriend has the magic touch."

Mac glanced sharply at her, worried that she might be criticizing the quickness with which Hailey had become a part of his and Julianna's life. Phoebe said nothing more, however, and in the interest of not borrowing trouble, he didn't ask her what she was thinking. Besides, this was his life, his kid. After urging him to meet someone and approving of Hailey before, Phoebe shouldn't criticize. And maybe she wasn't. Maybe Mac was reading something into her tone and her expression that simply wasn't there.

Hailey soon came out of the bedroom, hand-in-hand with Julianna, who was now fully decked-out in cape, ears, mask, and a big, big smile. She pranced around for her admiring audience. Greg called her a "Catwoman Princess." Phoebe gave her a special Halloween treat basket and earned an extra hug and a kiss. But it was Hailey that Julianna kept turning to, to retie her cape, to straighten her ears, to reassure her again and again that she was the best Catwoman ever.

His daughter, Mac realized, had fallen hard for Hailey.

Fallen as hard as he had.

The realization shouldn't have hit him like a brick. How else could he classify his feelings for this woman? For days he had thought about her even when he should have been concentrating on something else. He walked around in a state of near-constant arousal. He was living on caffeine and a maximum of four hours of sleep because he couldn't get enough of making love with her. The two of them were practically giddy over the discoveries they were making about one another.

He had wanted companionship, someone to laugh with again, and yes, someone to share his bed. But he had found giddiness, instead. And what more was waiting?

The question remained with him after saying goodbye to Phoebe and Greg, who, for some mysterious reason, seemed to be spending Halloween together. He thought about that as he walked with Hailey and Julianna to Katie's party.

The gala was an annual event, conducted in a spacious, converted loft filled with children, stuffed-sheet ghosts and glowing jack-o'-lanterns. Both Katie's mother and father were artists, friends of Eve's from way back. But until Mac walked through the door with Hailey on his arm, he hadn't stopped to think this might be awkward for her and for him. The adults in attendance were mainly other parents, a group who had all married and started families about the same time as Mac and Eve had. Many of these people had suffered along with Mac through Eve's illness and death. They were friends. It was perhaps natural that there be some hesitation as he introduced Hailey. He wasn't surprised that some of the women seemed to be sizing her up, that there was rank speculation from some of the men. He just wished he had thought about this before inviting her to come along.

Hailey met the group's subtle challenge with two solid defenses. First, she was sweet and loving to Julianna. And second, she was charming and yet forthright. Her demeanor said clearly, "This is me. And I'm with Mac. Accept me as I am." He only hoped they would.

The crowd swallowed up him and Hailey, separating them for a long while, until Mac saw her huddled with two women who had been especially close to Eve. He edged close, eavesdropping as he pretended to graze on the spread of goodies on a nearby table. He heard only laughter, followed by an invitation for him and Hailey to come to dinner next week.

Before Hailey made a reply, she looked up and caught him lurking. She pulled him, protesting, into the circle. "What do you think? Dinner next Friday with the Morrisons?"

He mumbled a tentative agreement. Hailey shot him a puzzled look, but was soon caught up in conversation again.

Mac sought out a quiet corner. At least as quiet as a man in a glowing yellow Joker suit could hope to find in a roomful of exuberant youngsters. He was angry at himself for feeling so confused. An hour ago he had been worried about these women being nice to Hailey. Now he was ticked off because they were inviting the two of them out as a couple.

A couple.

The word carried a hundred connotations.

None of which he felt ready to accept.

His name was called before he could give the matter too much thought, and he was pulled back into the merriment of the party. But soon after, he found his daughter and Hailey and suggested they leave. He said very little on the way home, letting Julianna fill the rather awkward silences with her chatter.

Once there, he and his daughter had a worse-than-usual tussle over bed. She was keyed up, still excited from the party, even after she had put on her pajamas and had been told to get into bed. But when Hailey suggested, rather sensibly, that Julianna stay up for a little while, Mac responded with a flat, perhaps harsher than necessary, denial.

Julianna stomped her foot and called him mean. Mac carried her, sobbing, to bed. He left her with her favorite doll and firm instructions not to get up.

Hailey was waiting for him in the living room, her brown eyes huge in a face that still bore faint traces of the whiskers she had drawn to complete her costume.

Jerking off his silly, green polka-dot bow tie, Mac stalked to the kitchen and threw it in the trash. He poured himself some bottled water, added ice, then held the glass to his suddenly aching head. Closing his eyes, he let the cold seep into his skull. He wanted to be numb. He didn't want to think. He especially didn't want to talk to Hailey.

But he heard her come in, and she was standing near the breakfast bar when he finally opened his eyes.

"Did I do something wrong?" she asked.

He didn't know what to say. She had been completely delightful to his friends and patient with his daughter and with him. How could he criticize her because all of a sudden he didn't know what he wanted?

"Mac?"

He took a deep breath. "I guess I'm just tired."

"And that's all?"

"Yes."

"You're sure?"

"That's what I said," he snapped, then immediately regretted his tone when she took a step back from him.

He saw her swallow hard before she said, "I'm sorry, Mac. I wasn't trying to be annoying."

"I know." He took a deep gulp of his water and wiped his mouth slowly with the back of his hand, trying to come up with exactly what he wanted to say. "I'm sorry, too. It's just been a long night."

She bit her bottom lip and hesitated a moment. "It wasn't easy to see me with Eve's friends, was it?"

Her perception shouldn't have surprised him. Someone as smart as Hailey had to have known what he was feeling when everyone at that party started looking at them. "Yeah," he admitted. "It was kind of difficult."

"I hope nothing I did made you or Julianna feel uncomfortable."

He shook his head. "It wasn't you. It was just me. It all kind of hit me tonight."

"All?"

"You and me."

She nodded. "We've been moving pretty fast."

"It does feel that way."

"So maybe we should take it down a notch or two."

An immediate and shockingly vehement, "No," escaped his lips.

Hailey looked every bit as confused as he felt. She shifted uncertainly from one foot to the other.

Setting his glass aside, Mac thrust an impatient hand through his hair. What did he want? He needed to figure that out. Pronto.

Early on, he had told Hailey he wasn't after just a warm body to fill a void in his life. That much still held true. He had wanted *her* body, *her* laughter, *her* company. What he hadn't anticipated, however, was how permanent this felt. The feeling of rightness that had accompanied their first lovemaking had swiftly permeated their entire relationship. He didn't know how to react. He had set out to find a *date,* not a wife, not a mother for his daughter.

The fact that he used the words wife and mother, even to himself, rocked him to his core.

"Maybe you're right," he said hastily. "We need to slow down."

Hailey was still watching him with an uncertain look in her eyes. "All right."

Mac cleared his throat. "This doesn't mean . . . that is to say . . . I'm not saying I don't want us to be together."

"Are you sure about that?"

"God, no."

And because he needed and wanted to touch her, Mac went to her, pulled her close. He knew it might be wiser to keep his distance. But she looked so vulnerable. He didn't want to hurt her. That was the last thing he had set out to do. Yet that was the whole problem. In getting involved with Hailey, he had set out with one goal in mind and found the reality to be something else entirely.

"I think I just need a little space," he whispered.

Her answer was a deep sigh.

"Okay?" He stepped back, tilting her face up to his with a gentle hand under her chin.

She studied him for what seemed like a long time. "Yes, I think you're right," she said at last.

"Please don't take this the wrong way."

"I'm not." She stepped back. "We have been intruding on each other's lives."

"Intruding?" He frowned. How exactly had he been intruding in on her life? Or maybe he should ask *who* he had been intruding on. He remembered the man's voice he had heard over her phone on Saturday night two weeks ago. It could have been a brother or a cousin, except he knew all of her relatives were in California. It might be a friend. That seemed plausible. And yet . . . worries he hadn't even considered began to plague him.

"I'm going home." Pressing a thoroughly impersonal kiss on his cheek, Hailey turned and headed for the living room, where she had left her cape.

"Wait a minute," Mac said, trailing after her. "It was cold on the way home from the party. Don't you want to borrow a sweater or coat?"

She swirled the cape around her shoulders and avoided his gaze. "I'm sure I'll be fine."

"Hailey." He caught her hand. "Don't leave just now."

"I thought that's what you wanted." Hurt flickered across her face before she brought her expression under careful control.

He closed his eyes, praying for guidance. "Please be patient with me."

Her mouth trembled; her eyes filled.

He stepped closer. "Please," he whispered before kissing her.

Hailey resisted at first. Then, with a sound that was half groan and half sob, she melted against him. She hated herself for being so malleable. But she understood the confusion Mac was experiencing. If she pushed too hard, he would either back away completely, or they would end up rushing headlong into a hasty, ill-fated relationship. God knew, she didn't need another one of those in her life. He was right to put the brakes on. She should be relieved instead of hurt. And yet . . .

She ached.

"I have to go," she told him, afraid she was going to do something stupid like cry. Clutching her cape around her, she headed for the door.

"I'll call you."

Not bothering to reply, she left, speeding down the stairs and out onto the street. And maybe it was her costume, maybe it was the cold air and the witchy feel of the Halloween night, but Hailey felt like howling at the big, yellow moon that floated high above the city lights.

Flowers arrived for Hailey promptly at 10:00 a.m. the next morning. Small and tastefully arranged, the autumn bouquet contained a card that read, "You were the first thing I thought of this morning."

The message was written in Mac's own irregular scrawl. But neither the sentiment nor the chrysanthemum blooms of yellow, crimson and bronze did much to ease the wistfulness inside her.

Over lunch, Pam told her to chill. "This is a typical male thing that's happening with Mac. He's holding you close, but pushing you away at the same time. You know the drill."

Hailey hated describing as a "drill" what had been happening between her and Mac. Her foolish, romantic nature had overruled the caution she should have exercised. She knew she had screwed up, big-time. But damn it, before last night, she had begun to hope they might be onto something magical and real. She guessed the deflation she felt right now was what she got for hoping.

"Let's be clear about this," Pam continued in her usual crisp and businesslike tones. "It's perfectly normal for a man to suddenly need space after he's bedded you."

Choking on a mouthful of salad, Hailey croaked out, *"Bedded?"*

Pam nodded solemnly. "That's how men view it, you know. It's a throwback to cavemen days."

"But *bedded?"* Hailey repeated. "That's archaic. I'm shocked that you would even use the term."

"I'm only being realistic." Pam patted her hand. "To men, you and I and other women are just so much chattel."

Hailey couldn't have been more astonished if Pam had suddenly sprouted alien antennae. "I don't agree. Most of the men I've known—including Mac—are much more enlightened than that."

"And I guess it was enlightened of him to request some space one night and then send you flowers the next morning?"

"The request for space was probably sensible," Hailey retorted defensively. "The flowers are sweet."

Arching one eyebrow, Pam merely speared a chunk of avocado from her own salad.

"At least he picked out the flowers himself this time."

"But *why* did he send them? That's the real question."

"He said why. Because he was thinking of me."

Pam tsk-tsked. "You are so blind, Hailey. No wonder you were so worried about undertaking a transitional relationship with this man. Have you no judgment, no control?''

The reminder that this had started out as a temporary dating experience made Hailey squirm. She could imagine Pam's horror if she was told Hailey had fallen in love with Mac.

In love with a man who needed space. Just her luck.

Tapping her fork thoughtfully against the edge of her plate, Pam stared off into space. "The important thing to consider now is how you're going to handle this."

"I don't see what there is to handle."

"Oh, really? Then what are you going to do when he calls you?"

The problem Hailey feared was that he wouldn't call her. "I don't know."

"He will call," Pam insisted. "Probably with some sort of wildly romantic invitation."

"How do you know this?"

"I'm older than you. And I've just finished reading this wonderful article called "Male on the Prowl." It provided some incredible insights into the male psyche and just confirmed what experience had already told me."

"And what's that?"

Eyes alight with diabolical glee, Pam leaned forward. "Men are like animals. They love to play with their prey."

Hailey's mouth dropped open. "You have truly lost it this time, my friend."

"Just listen a minute. Men are always complaining about women playing games."

"True."

"But who is it that forces us into those games?" Pam ticked off reasons with well-manicured fingers. "Men don't call us when they say they will. They don't show up on time. They don't remember special occasions."

"Some men don't," Hailey corrected her.

"Most men," the other woman insisted. "And so, in order to get along with them, we must resort to feminine wiles. To trickery. To playing hard to get. To second-guessing."

"I hate all those things."

Pam sniffed. "Which brings us back to my original question. What are you going to do when Mac calls you?"

"It depends."

"On what?"

"On what he says." Hailey threw down her napkin, rapidly reaching the end of her patience with this conversation. "Let's just drop this. Mac may not call. I may not hear from him for a while. I'm certainly not calling him."

"Mmm," Pam murmured in a way that conveyed her complete disbelief.

Mac didn't call. At least not that afternoon. Or that night. Or Saturday, either. Hailey was forced into calling the phone company and asking that her line be checked for defects. Of course there was no problem. Except that maybe it was Mac's line that was out.

Hailey punched in the number and hung up when he answered, her cheeks flaming.

She supposed she was just going to have to bide her time.

Quickly dialing another number, she waited until Pam's voice came on the line. "All right, tell me again, when do you think Mac's going to call? And what kind of wildly romantic invitation am I supposed to resist?"

8

Mac was having a difficult time with Monday morning's show. Not that the subject matter was dull. They had managed to snare a visit from the gubernatorial candidate who had surged in the polls for the upcoming election. The fact that the guest's ultra-right views contrasted sharply with the liberal leanings of Mac's boss, Day Varner, should have created fireworks. And maybe it had. Mac's difficulty was he couldn't concentrate on anything that was being said.

Sitting just outside the glass broadcast booth, not three feet from a man who could become New York's governor in less than a week, would have been an adrenaline boost just a month ago. Mac couldn't figure out exactly why he had the blahs. Maybe it was because everything was gray. His suit. The November sky on the walk to work this morning. The carpet on the walls around them. He needed a shot of color.

He needed Hailey.

The candidate was enlarging on his plan to get state spending under control without cutting crucial services, and Day was pressing him on every point. Mac sensed the atmosphere getting hot.

But the only heat he was interested in was of an intimate nature. Hailey would know just how to fan it into flames.

Someone tapped Mac on the shoulder, and Sylvia bent close to whisper, "Do you think Day should attack quite so hard?"

Sitting up, Mac caught his boss's eye and gave him the signal to cool it down. Day relied on Mac for such directives, as when he warmed to a subject, he had a tendency to rush off on nonproductive tangents. Now he switched topics and went to the phones so that both their loyal and not-so-loyal listeners would have a chance to ask their own questions.

Mac managed to stay on top of what was happening for the last half hour of the day's program. Their esteemed guest was whisked on his way to his next appearance, and there was a brief conference about tomorrow's program. Then Mac sought out Sylvia and asked her to come into his office.

"Thanks for being on your toes in there," he told his cherubic assistant. "I sure wasn't."

Her smile was smug. "You're in a funk. You've been in a funk ever since Halloween."

"Have I?" Mac pretended an interest in the notes on the clipboard he held. Sylvia was right, but he wasn't going to give her the satisfaction of agreeing with her.

"It's because of Hailey."

Mac didn't dignify that assertion with a reply.

"I can't believe how you're treating her."

He couldn't resist clarifying that. "We both decided we needed some breathing room."

"Is that why you sent her flowers again this morning?"

"How did you know that?" The woman was an amazing snoop. If she tired of this job, he knew she'd make it with the CIA.

Sylvia dropped a message memo onto the clipboard. "The florist called in the middle of the show, to check the order. You told them to make sure this morning's arrangement to Miss Hailey Porter was different than the one sent on Friday. Only their computer has malfunctioned and they couldn't remember what they sent last week."

"Hell," Mac said, momentarily forgetting to pretend the flowers were no big deal. "So what have they done, not sent anything?"

"I took care of it," Sylvia soothed. "I called Hailey's associate—"

"You what?"

"I called Ms. Witherspoon, and she told me all about the Friday arrangement. Then I called the florist and made sure you sent something a little softer this time."

"And what did I send?" Mac asked, dreading to hear.

A dreamy look drifted across his assistant's face. "Just three perfect pink roses."

Having just paid the bill for the first floral extravaganza Sylvia had ordered, Mac was both pleased and surprised. "Sounds nice."

"At first I thought Ms. Witherspoon was wrong to suggest—"

"Wait a minute," Mac cut in. "Hailey's partner suggested the roses?"

"Well, of course." Sylvia placed both hands on her rounded hips. "Does three roses sound like something I would come up with? As Phoebe always says, I don't have a gift for understatement."

"Oh, forget Phoebe." With a disgusted sigh, Mac dropped into his desk chair.

"My, my," Sylvia murmured, folding her arms across her midriff. "Someone's mood is awfully foul."

"Well, this is all Phoebe's fault."

"What?"

"If she hadn't made that remark about Hailey—"

"I had brunch with both of you yesterday, and all she did was urge you to call Hailey. That's all any of us did."

"It wasn't anything she said yesterday."

"Then when? What did she say?"

Mac waved off her questions. "It doesn't matter now. Just something Phoebe said got me thinking that Hailey and I were moving too fast."

"So you broke it off with her based on some offhand statement from Phoebe." Sylvia's tone conveyed her utter disbelief.

Head beginning to pound, Mac let his voice rise. "How many times do I have to tell you people that I didn't break anything off? Would I be sending flowers to someone I didn't want to see again?"

Spots of color appeared in Sylvia's cheeks. "Don't yell at me, Mac Williams."

"I'm not yelling. I'm explaining."

"But you're explaining to the wrong woman. Let me get Hailey on the phone."

"No!"

"Mac—"

"No, no and no again," he repeated. "Now go do something productive."

Sylvia strode to the door with as much authority as a five-foot-one munchkin could convey. "You'd better watch out. Ms. Witherspoon told me that any time I thought about looking for a new job, I could talk to her."

"That's fine," Mac said. "Go work for them. I don't care."

The door closed behind his assistant with a firm little click. Mac counted to ten, balled up the message from the florist and threw it across the room. At the moment he wished Sylvia was working with Hailey. Perhaps then he'd have some clue as to what was happening with her. With Sylvia's expert espionage ability, there'd be nothing he wouldn't know.

He had expected Hailey to call Friday morning after she got the flowers. When she didn't, he even called the florist to make sure the delivery had been made. But he'd heard nothing all that day or the next.

By Saturday night he had been so miserable that he had gone out with Greg. What a disaster. Mac was seriously beginning to question the foundation of his three closest friendships. Phoebe disapproved of him.

Sylvia wanted to control him. And he and Greg didn't seem to communicate the way they used to.

They had gone to a bar. To meet women. At least that was Mac's expectation. In his younger days, whenever a woman had started to get too close, as Hailey had, he and Greg used to go out on the prowl. Mac hadn't been looking for sex, like he had when he was in college and such unions didn't require a health card. But he had wondered if a few hours with an attractive woman other than Hailey might clear his perspective a bit. Greg, who used to be a "babe magnet," had pooped out on him, finding something wrong with every woman they met. The two of them were home by eleven, and then Greg had hung around, crashing on the couch like he hadn't since Eve started kicking him out years and years ago.

There was something going on with Greg, Mac thought, something pretty bad if he didn't want to discuss it with his best friend. But he didn't spend his entire weekend worrying about Greg.

Sunday, when he had really wanted to call Hailey, Mac called Krystal, the young dancer Greg had set him up with before. They'd had a drink early Sunday evening. It wasn't so bad. They had made plans to have dinner this Saturday. Mac supposed he should be pleased with himself. He was just doing what everyone had said he should in the beginning—getting back out there. No one had advised him to become fixated on one woman. That couldn't be healthy for him right now, anyway. He needed to play the field. He would enjoy playing it. Sunday, Krystal had been even more beautiful than he remembered.

But she wasn't Hailey.

No one had her zest.

Or her laughter.

Or her legs.

Or her . . .

Before he could run through her many features and talents, Mac swore, "Damn it all to hell." He punched a button on his phone. "Sylvia?"

She answered with a cold, "Yes, Mr. Williams."

"Cut the crap and get that Ms. Witherspoon on the phone."

There was a pause, then a snappy, "Right away, sir!"

With an irritated frown, Hailey pushed through the doors of the Plaza Hotel and looked around for Pam. Just after Hailey's lunch with a client, her partner had rung her cellular phone and said to meet her in the lobby of the Plaza at two. She wouldn't say why, except that it was important. It was five after the hour now, and Hailey saw no sign of Pam.

As she looked around for a seat, she was paged. There was a call for her on the house phones. She dialed the appropriate number and said wearily, "Yes, Pam."

"How did you know it would be me?"

"Just luck, I guess. What's going on?"

"Well, the thing is . . . Mac called."

Hailey's heart fluttered in an utterly foolish way. "Called you? Why?"

"He's waiting at the hotel for you."

"You're kidding?"

"No, and while I hate to say I told you so . . ."

"Stop gloating." Hailey was craning her neck, looking for Mac. "Why did he call you?"

"Perhaps because he was afraid he couldn't get through to you otherwise." Pam chuckled. "My dear, you have this man on the run."

"That's not what I want."

"But it should be."

"Stop it, please. Now where is Mac supposed to be?"

Pam explained that Mac had elicited her help in a ruse to get her to the hotel. "Just ask for me at the front desk."

"For you? Why?"

"Mac's wonderful assistant and I put this whole thing together. I was supposed to tell you this was some business meeting that had been set up in a hurry by one of our clients. Mac's expecting you to be surprised."

"Oh, really?"

"I told him I would keep this on the qt, but I couldn't do that to you. Just in case you don't want to see him."

Hailey paused. "You think I shouldn't?"

"That's not my decision."

"But if you were me?"

Hesitating only a beat, Pam said, "I might see what sort of wildly romantic afternoon he was planning to offer." She cleared her throat. "I mean, I've never been one to pass up a little romp now and then."

"You are such a fraud, Pam Witherspoon."

"Now, why would you say that?"

Hailey tucked a strand of hair behind her ear. "All that talk about men playing with their prey and how I should *handle* Mac."

"So I like a little caveman activity occasionally. Sue me."

"Goodbye, Pam."

Her friend merely laughed and promised, "I'll hold down the fort while you frolic."

Hailey stared at the receiver for a moment, replaced it, then leaned against the elegantly papered wall, considering her options.

When the knock he was expecting came, Mac was waiting anxiously by the door of the suite. Hailey stood just outside, her navy suit jacket slung over her shoulder, one hand on her hip and a distinctly unsurprised look on her face.

"Pam told you," he said.

"She's a good friend, and you've got some nerve."

He stepped back as Hailey sailed past. "Nerve, huh?"

In the center of the room, she swung around to face him. "Yes, nerve. You brush me off, then try for a quickie at a hotel."

"Wait a minute. I did not brush you off. This is not a quickie setup."

"It feels that way."

He closed the door, then raked a hand through his hair. "I'm sorry. I don't have any excuses about how I acted on Halloween. I just got..." His explanation ended in a shrug he knew was pathetic.

Hailey threw her jacket down on the tapestry-upholstered settee in front of the window. She glanced back at Mac, then tossed her briefcase and purse on the coat. "I am so angry about this. Embarrassed, too. Here you complain about your friends scheming against you, then you get my friend to help trick me into an afternoon at a hotel. How mortifying."

"Excuse me," he retorted, drawing himself up. "But your friend Pam didn't seem the least bit shocked about this. I just wanted to see you. I thought this would be neutral ground."

"Why didn't you just call?"

"I was afraid you wouldn't talk to me. You didn't call me after I sent flowers. Twice."

"Because I didn't know what those flowers meant. I thought they might be pity presents."

He stepped toward her, frowning. "Pity presents? What in God's name is that?"

"I don't know. It doesn't matter now." She folded her arms across her stomach. "So what did you want to say to me?"

He choked. "I don't know."

"Mac!"

"I know, I know." Flinging himself down in a nearby chair, he rubbed a hand along his jaw. "I'm a first-class jerk, aren't I?"

Hailey threw up her hands. "Well, if you're going to choose a hotel to *not* talk in, the Plaza is as close as it gets to first class."

The glimmer of amusement he detected in her tone was encouraging. "It is a beautiful room, isn't it?"

"I suppose."

"Have you ever stayed here?"

"No."

"Neither have I."

They both fell silent then. Hailey began to tap her foot.

Mac braced his hands on his thighs and asked, "Do you want to leave?"

"If you don't have anything to say..." She waited for a moment, then let out an irritated sigh and turned to pick up her things.

She was at the door when Mac sprang into action, taking her arm and making her turn around to face him.

She protested, pulling back.

But he wouldn't let her go. "I do have a few things to say."

She stopped struggling and gazed steadily back at him. "I'm listening."

"I don't know what I'm feeling, Hailey. I'm confused. That's why I acted like a jackass. The only thing I'm sure of is...is that I want to figure this out."

"Figure what out?"

"Us."

"You think an afternoon of sex in a fancy hotel room will do that?"

"Of course not. If this were just about sex it would be a lot easier."

She hesitated, then agreed, "You're right."

He lifted his hand to her hair, stroked his fingers through the shining, pale waves. "Please, Hailey. Just bear with me on this. Don't be angry. Try to be patient. There's a lot I'm trying to work out."

Hailey had always known she was a softie and a pushover. But she had never considered herself a masochist until now, as she considered staying here with Mac. Damn it, how many times did she have to go through the same lessons before they sunk in?

The answers eluded her. Especially when Mac kissed her.

Breaking away from his embrace, she said, "You know something, Mr. Williams? You have the most persuasive kiss in the world. If we bottled it, there's every reason to think we could achieve world peace."

His laughter was deep. "Your kiss isn't so bad, either."

"Really?" Dropping her things on the floor at her sides, Hailey pressed her mouth to his once again.

She kissed him until there was nothing to consider but her arousal. And his. Nothing to contemplate but the hows and whys of getting her panties off and his pants unzipped, finding a condom and getting him inside her. He brought her to orgasm once against the wall beside the door. Once on the floor. And once, much later, in the big, firm bed in the suite's bedroom.

When the autumn sunlight began to fade, they shared a naked picnic of expensive room-service sandwiches, chocolate-dipped fruit and champagne. Pleasurably tender in all the right places, Hailey slipped her body over his, taking him deep inside her while his torso strained up to meet hers. They rocked together, without urgency, their gazes unwaveringly joined. Her climax was sweeter, easier than the earlier explosions of passion. Yet in its subtlety she found even more power, more emotion.

The last tremors were moving through her when Mac's completion came. She loved looking into his eyes, watching them widen and close, feeling the way his muscular body went taut and then loose. The lazy way he smiled at her when it was over.

This was the sort of moment when people could blurt out all kinds of confessions. Hailey wanted to say she loved him. Here, when they were so in sync, when it seemed impossible that they would ever want to be anywhere but together. She wanted him to know how she felt.

But she couldn't put that pressure on him. He had said he was confused, that he needed her time and patience. She had to give him that. In waiting, she had nothing left to risk, for he already held her heart.

Didn't he know? she wondered as he slept beside her. Couldn't he feel how deeply she cared?

Phoebe was staying with Julianna, and if they wanted, they had the whole night to luxuriate in this room. About nine, however, Hailey suggested they go home—to his place.

"So you'll be there when Julianna wakes up to-morrow."

"She'll be fine without me for one night."

"I know...but it seems selfish when we're only blocks away."

"Then you have to stay with me all night."

"Mac—"

"Julianna's been asking for you. You could make her pancakes in the morning, like you did when I was sick."

"And what happens when she's fourteen and wants to sleep with her boyfriend, just like you did with me?"

"I'll lock her in her room."

Laughing, Hailey tossed a pillow at him, but stopped arguing. Julianna was his daughter, and this was his decision. There was nothing wrong with Julianna seeing them being loving and close. If this were casual, a fleeting liaison, she might feel differently. But it wasn't that. No matter that Mac wasn't quite sure of his feelings for her, this couldn't be called casual.

Hailey needed clothes for work in the morning. They walked to her place because it was a beautiful night and their spirits were soaring as high as the stars over the city. Cold and crisp, the air sparkled just like the feelings inside Hailey. At the corner across from her building, she turned, laughing at Mac's assertion that someone had already placed a Christmas tree high in a window above them.

While she stepped away from him, demanding that he point out the window, Mac saw a shadow surge toward them from the left. Instinctively he stepped toward Hailey, but he was too late. The shadow, which was a man, grabbed Hailey's arm. She screamed and struggled, though Mac yelled for her to stop. Metal flashed in the streetlights, and Hailey went down. Her assailant was already running away before Mac dropped to her side.

He couldn't breathe. For one, long, horrible moment, he thought she was dead and he couldn't move. It wasn't fair, he told himself.

Not Hailey, God. Don't put me through this again.

That prayer ran through him like a flash fire. Then he grabbed her, searching for the knife wound he was sure she had. All the while he pleaded with her to move, to tell him where she was hurt.

Her eyelids fluttered open. She stared at him, then pushed his hands away. "That creep got my purse. He cut the strap."

"Who cares? Are you okay?"

"I've never been mugged before."

Her outrage might have been comical. But Mac couldn't laugh. Light-headed with relief and another emotion he didn't care to examine, he gathered Hailey close in his arms.

9

—→←—

As he watched Hailey sharing pancakes with Julianna in the weak light of the November morning, Mac admitted to himself what he hadn't been able to face last night. He had made a terrible, awful mistake. He had opened a door that should have remained closed. He had let Hailey into his life, although he wasn't sure that was what he wanted.

"You're going to be late for work," she said, smiling at him, looking unaware of his inner turmoil.

"I wanted to make sure you were really okay."

"Of course I am. Just a little sore."

"Were you scared?" Julianna asked for perhaps the fifth time. She had awakened last night when Hailey and Mac arrived home, and it had been impossible to keep what had happened from her. Though Mac wanted Julianna to feel safe, he also wanted to be honest about some of the dangers the city presented.

Hailey ruffled her hair. "I was just mad, sweetie pie. I was really furious at that man for getting my purse."

"You shouldn't have struggled," Mac said.

"As I've told you nine thousand times, it was instinctive."

"But you could have been hurt."

Glancing toward Julianna, whose eyes had grown wide, Hailey said, "Let's not rehash this, okay?"

Mac told Julianna to finish her meal. He washed sticky syrup from her face, then found her jacket and his briefcase and sent her in search of a book for "sharing time" at pre-school. Hailey, who was still in his old flannel bathrobe, sat drinking coffee at the table. No matter that she said she was fine, she was pale. She also had an ugly, purpling bruise up her left arm where the mugger had grabbed her.

"Do you think you're going in to work?" Mac asked her.

"Of course."

"Just take your time."

"I will." She pushed away from the table and stood gingerly. "I'm going back over to my place first. I forgot some papers I need for work. I guess I'll need a key for here."

"A key?" Mac stared at her blankly. "What for?"

"To lock the door when I leave."

"Just lock it behind you."

"But the deadbolt—"

"We'll take a chance today, all right?" He kissed her goodbye, then called for Julianna and left.

Hailey remained rooted to the same spot. Mac hadn't wanted to give her a key. Even temporarily. It was silly to be so hurt over something so trivial. But after yesterday, after last night, when he had clutched her to him, she had imagined things would be different. No, that wasn't exactly right. She had assumed many things had changed, but Mac hadn't said anything to tell her that was so. So they'd shared another incredible evening of sex. So he had been frightened when she was hurt. That proved nothing. All this morning, he had been so detached. Almost as bad as he had been last week after the Halloween party.

She told herself not to worry. She went to the office, had a busy day. Mac called her midway through the afternoon suggesting plans for the evening. She was reassured. Until she saw him. Until he was so polite, so remote, so completely controlled.

And yet he made love to her that night with the same heat, the same tenderness, as always.

She felt like a rat in a maze, running down one blind alley after another. By week's end she was worn out and afraid that at any moment she was going to make demands that Mac had already told her he couldn't meet just yet.

Friday evening, Greg, Phoebe and Sylvia came over for dinner. Hailey wanted to beg off, but Julianna pleaded with her to be there, and there wasn't much she could deny that child.

Besides, Hailey liked them all. Sylvia with her warm, open smile. Phoebe, so proper. Greg, who tried so hard to play the laconic. Hailey wondered if Phoebe knew Greg was in love with her. It wasn't easy to see if Mac's auburn-haired sister-in-law returned Greg's feelings. But there was definite tension of a sexual nature between the two. Sitting back, with a near-stranger's objectivity, Hailey could see clearly what was probably hidden from Mac and Sylvia.

Hailey thought they all liked her. Only from Phoebe did she pick up on any reserve. She couldn't tell if that was just the woman's nature or if she disapproved in any way of her, if that might be the source of some of Mac's hesitations.

After their spaghetti dinner, she and Phoebe volunteered to put away leftovers and load the dishwasher. The silence between them was comfortable, not strained, and Hailey told herself to stop worrying.

When the room was tidied and they started to join the others in the living room, Phoebe stopped her. "I'm glad Mac's found you, Hailey."

"So you approve of me."

Phoebe frowned. "That's not exactly what I meant. Mac doesn't need my approval. What I meant to say was, that I like you. I like how good you are to Julianna and to Mac."

Hailey wondered if Phoebe might shed some light on Mac's moodiness. Hesitantly she said, "I'll be honest. There are times when I'm not sure where I stand with Mac." She laughed mirthlessly. "Most of the time, as a matter of fact."

"Please remember what he's been through."

"I know."

"Mac doesn't love easily or lightly. When you're that sort of person, you don't let go easily, either."

Hailey was thinking she would never be able to compete with Eve, if it were her memory that was preventing Mac from loving her. But that wasn't what Phoebe meant.

To Phoebe's credit, she chose her words carefully. "I think it will be difficult for Mac to let himself care that much again. It's not Eve that would hold him back. It's himself." Phoebe reached out and squeezed Hailey's hand. "Hang in there. Have patience."

Her words were an echo of what Mac had said himself. Hailey knew this was wise counsel. She wished she weren't so impatient. What she wished more than anything, however, was that she hadn't fallen so hard and so fast for this man. It was as if the relationship was struggling to keep up with her emotions.

Standing in the doorway to the kitchen, studying the somber set of Mac's profile, Hailey understood why he had asked for some space last week. She thought she needed some herself.

She struggled to put a light note in her voice. "You know something, guys, I'm beat."

"No wonder," Greg said. "It's not every week that you get your purse cut off your body."

"And get knocked onto the pavement," Sylvia added. "You probably need to sleep for about twenty-four hours."

"Do you want someone to go home with you?" Phoebe asked, looking worried.

"Of course not. I'll be fine."

Mac got to his feet. "Are you sure you have to go?"

Hailey told herself she didn't hear relief in his voice. Ignoring him, she smiled at Phoebe, whose forehead was still creased with concern. She held out her arms to Julianna and scooped her up, welcoming the solid weight of her little body.

Hugging her tight, Hailey said, "You be a good girl when it's time for bed, okay? Give your old dad a break."

"I'll try," Julianna agreed. She leaned her forehead against Hailey's and whispered, "Will you be here tomorrow?"

"I don't think so," Hailey whispered back.

"The next day?"

"We'll see."

The small, chubby arms crept around her neck. "I like it when you're here."

"And I like being with you, too, sweetie pie."

Feeling absurdly like crying, Hailey set her down and called out goodbyes as she headed toward the door. Mac trailed her, standing silently by as she collected her coat and purse. Then he followed her out into the hall and shut the door behind him.

He rubbed a gentle hand up and down the arm that had been bruised. "You okay?"

"Very tired."

"You told Julianna we won't see you tomorrow."

"Don't you think that's for the best right now?"

He looked down at his shoes.

"Mac, I know I need to be patient. But something's wrong. Something's bothering you. And I'd like you to talk it out with me."

"I can't." Shoving his hands into his pockets, he shook his head. "Not now."

"Call me when you can."

"And not before?"

She closed her eyes. "I hate ultimatums. I don't believe in them."

She left it at that, left Mac standing there. He felt as if he was bleeding to death. Because he was falling in love with her, and he didn't want to. He couldn't, he told himself. Last night, when he was afraid Hailey was hurt, he remembered the helplessness of watching Eve die. Strong as his love for his wife had been, it hadn't been enough to hold her here. And he just couldn't go through that again.

Back inside, he was greeted by four sets of bassett-hound sad eyes. "Don't start," he told them all, glaring even at Julianna.

For once, they all did as he asked. His friends left, and his daughter went to bed without protest. Mac was glad. He'd had it with their advice, their prying, their know-it-all looks.

Mac needed to be alone. He had to think this thing with Hailey through. His responsibilities were to himself and to Julianna. He didn't want to screw up. Maybe the worst mistake he could make would be letting Hailey go. Or perhaps, it would be easier that way. If he stayed involved with her, if he let himself fall the rest of the way in love with her, then he would have some tremendous highs. Having known a powerful love, he knew the joy that might be his and Hailey's. But he also knew the lows. The gut-wrenching awful pits of despair.

Was it a crime to opt for the even keel?

* * *

In the coffee shop down the street from the converted brownstone Pam had received as a divorce settlement a decade before, Hailey sipped a double-Dutch-chocolate cappuccino. Outside, a late afternoon winter rain was falling. The dreary cityscape matched the echoing emptiness of her heart.

"Oh, my." Pam heaved a sigh and pushed her own double latte aside. "I guess it's true. There is no such thing as a transitional relationship."

Hailey focused heavy eyes on her friend. "What?"

"I was hoping you would prove an exception," Pam continued. "But the fact that you've fallen in love with Mac only goes to prove that the two terms are simply incompatible. The word relationship implies something lasting. Temporary, transitional—those words just don't fit, do they?"

After taking a much-needed gulp of chocolate and caffeine, Hailey said, "I certainly wish you had said this to me about a month ago. I might not be feeling so bad."

"Don't kid yourself. If you hadn't fallen in love with Mac Williams, it would have been someone else. You're just the sort of woman who falls, Hailey." Settling her chin on her palm, Pam added, ever so softly, "Maybe we're all that sort of woman."

Hailey made no reply. Pam was right about the ridiculousness of transitional relationships. But she was dead wrong about there being someone else out there like Mac. If there was one thing the past month had done for Hailey, it had restored her belief in the power of fate.

It had been fate that Mac had found her old phone number, fate that had brought them together again and again. And perhaps fate was even now working out the solution to this mess.

Something about that last statement didn't seem just right, but Hailey was too tired, too dispirited to try to puzzle it through just now.

Sighing again, she turned from her contemplation of the soggy street and looked around the restaurant. It was filled with people, no doubt due to the rain.

Across from the tiny table she and Pam were occupying sat a young couple. They were talking in low voices to one another. Occasionally, their hands would brush. Then one of them would laugh. Nervously. The very air around them was crackling with electricity.

Hailey managed to smile, thinking that the two of them could have been her and Mac eight years ago. Both of them so intense, so eager to impress the other, so aware that if they followed their impulses they would set off a huge chain of events.

She wished they had. She wished with all her heart that she had taken Mac up to her bed that night so long ago. If only she hadn't sat back, hadn't waited on . . . fate.

Sitting up, Hailey took a deep breath.

Pam studied her in alarm. "What's wrong?"

"I just realized. I'm sitting here, waiting, when I should be doing something about this."

"But, Hailey, honey, Mac asked for some time, some patience."

"That's such bull. Either you love someone or you don't, Pam."

"I don't know if it's that simple—"

"Yes, it is. The problems come when we all start making it so complicated. Before we even get into the thing, we start being afraid of getting hurt."

"It's human nature to guard your heart."

Eyes widening, Hailey shook her head. "That's dead wrong. It's human nature to open your heart."

Gathering up umbrella and raincoat, she pushed back her chair and left with a mumbled, "I've got to go see Mac."

She ran two blocks through the rain before she thought to catch a taxi. Then she ran three blocks more when an accident slowed traffic before the cab could get her to Mac's place. So she was drenched when she rang his doorbell. But he was, too, dripping wet and wrapped in his old robe, right out of the shower.

Without waiting to consider her actions, Hailey threw herself into his arms.

He kicked the door shut. "What is it? What's wrong?"

She struggled to catch her breath. "Nothing."

"But you've been running."

"Because I had to tell..." Her voice faltered as she faced him, then strengthened as her resolve returned. "I had to tell you that I love you, Mac."

She saw the muscles work in his throat as he swallowed.

"It's okay," she assured him. "You don't have to say it to me. You don't even have to feel it right now. That's not why I'm telling you."

"But, Hailey, I—"

"No, no," she cut in, silencing him. "Don't do that. Don't say anything you're not sure you feel. Just... don't shut me out, either. Don't close yourself off from your feelings."

"You don't understand," he began again.

"But I do. You're afraid to love anyone else again. That's how I was from the start with you. I don't know, maybe I fell in love with you eight years ago and never completely recovered."

He looked pained.

She waved aside his protests. "It's okay. That doesn't matter. What I was trying to get to was that I knew right from the minute that we re-met that I *could* love you. I wanted to. I wanted to love Julianna, too. And yet I knew I could get hurt. All the risks were so clear." She paused to suck in another lungful of air. "I haven't really told you about my marriage, Mac. You know Jonathan had two boys?"

He nodded. "And I know you love them a lot. I just haven't been able to piece together what happened."

"He went back to his first wife, to Trevor and Luke's mother. In England. He took the boys away from me." Tears she thought had long since been cried out gathered in her eyes. "I loved them so much, Mac. I didn't love Jonathan, not enough to stay married to him, but those boys..." She bit her lip to stop its trembling. "In all the ways that mattered, they were my children. But I had to let them go. It was the best thing for them. But it nearly destroyed me."

A dull ache pulsed deep in Mac's gut as he considered how it would feel to never see his little girl again. Now he knew the source of the sadness that came over Hailey every time she spoke of her stepsons.

"When I realized your situation..." She stopped to brush the tears that had joined the rain on her cheeks. "I didn't even want to know you, much less Julianna. But then I stayed here that night you were sick, and she was so wonderful. And I couldn't stay away from you. And now...now I love you. Both of you."

Mac was working hard, trying to resist the emotions she was arousing in him. She had seen through his smoke screens. By expressing her own fears, she was giving voice to his. With those barriers out in the open, kicking them aside seemed much more possible, more desirable. If only he could let himself go, let himself believe he could have another miracle in his life. If only he knew he could be strong enough to face whatever came with the love he wanted to give Hailey.

She read his struggles all too well. Stepping into his arms again, she said, "I know we could hurt each other, Mac. But it could be good, too. And if we don't try, if you don't meet me halfway, then how will we ever live with not knowing? Remember last time? We left everything up to fate." She laughed. "I don't know about you, but I'm not willing to do that again."

"Of course you're right," he murmured. "Of course we have to find out."

His mouth was lowering toward hers when the doorbell pealed.

"Ignore it," he said, kissing her.

But the ringing went on. Then someone knocked. A woman called Mac's name.

Krystal.

Too late, Mac remembered the date he had made last weekend. With everything that had happened since Monday, he had completely forgotten. "I can explain this," he said to Hailey before opening the door.

But there Krystal stood. In the same short, tight black dress that he remembered from their first date. Her smile was wide, brilliantly white, but it faded quickly as her gaze swung from Mac to Hailey and then back again.

"What's going on?" she demanded.

Hailey didn't wait to hear. Mac called after her. Her steps didn't falter. If he let her go this time, there'd be no turning back. And that was more than he could bear.

Leaving Krystal open-mouthed and sputtering, he ran after Hailey. Down the stairs and out into the street, with his robe flapping, his feet bare and his hair still wet. He chased her as he should have done eight years ago and as he should have chased her every time she had tried to escape him since. This time, he caught her. He made her look at him. And, because it seemed as if the situation warranted a grand gesture, he went down on his knee in front of her.

"That woman is nothing to me," he said with all the sincerity he could muster. "She's someone I was trying to use to forget you. I had forgotten she was even coming over."

"Fine. Go back to her." Hailey tried to jerk away, but he held her steady.

"I don't want to. I don't want her. Or anyone else. I only want you." He gripped her hand as hard as he could. "I don't want to love you, Hailey. I've tried not to. But I'm not sure I can stop it from happening. I'm not sure it would be right to try and stop it."

"Don't do this," Hailey said, closing her eyes. "Don't say things you don't mean."

"Hailey, if I didn't mean any of this, would I be out here dressed this way? If I didn't care, it'd be a helluva lot easier just to let you go."

For the first time since bursting into his apartment, she looked at him, really looked. She took in his short, barely decent robe and his dignity-shattering pose. But most of all, she saw the sincerity in his hazel eyes. From the moment they had met, she had admired the strength of character revealed by his steady, clear gaze.

"Get up," she muttered.

His jaw setting in a stubborn line, he stayed as he was.

"Get up, please. And hug me."

He got to his feet and enclosed her in his arms. Only then did Hailey realize a crowd had gathered around them. A New York City street crowd, the sort the world thought of as impersonal and uncaring. Smashing stereotypes, they cheered as Mac kissed her.

And behind his back, in her tight, black dress, stood the woman who had appeared at Mac's door. Hailey caught the brief flicker of yearning in her eyes. Then, grudgingly the woman smiled, gracefully accepting defeat.

Hailey reciprocated and lifted a prayer that neither she nor that dress would show up again.

Epilogue

Snow began to fall as Mac made his way down the street outside his home. Julianna bobbed along at his side, chattering excitedly about something she wanted to show Hailey. They were late coming home from school and work, and Hailey would be waiting. After moving in this past weekend, she had taken today off from work to get the rest of her things settled in the condo.

Mac told himself this arrangement would be no different from the way they had lived for the past few months. Hailey had spent more time with him and Julianna than at her place. But this was permanent. As solid and real as the engagement ring he had slipped on her finger last week. Thinking of the wedding they planned for the spring made him climb the three flights of stairs at top speed.

"Do I get to be in the wedding?" Julianna asked, though she knew the answer by heart.

"Of course," Mac answered patiently as he unlocked their door.

"And I can sprinkle rose petals down the aisle?" This flower-throwing thing had really caught her imagination.

Mac tickled her chin. "I'll get you a bushel of rose petals if you want."

"Cool!" she shouted, and ran down the hall, calling Hailey's name.

He took off his coat, followed Julianna and found Hailey sitting cross-legged in the middle of the bed. *Their* bed. The one that no longer felt so strange to him, especially when he awoke with her beside him.

When Julianna had finished with her tale of rose petals and school and what Katie and every one of her other friends had done and said, she scampered out of the room. Hailey held up a small black book. "What is this?" she demanded of Mac.

Surprised and delighted, he snatched it away. "This is very valuable. And I thought I had lost it again."

"I just found it in the bookcase," Hailey said, nodding toward the shelves beside the bed. "And it looks like some bachelor's date book. Is it yours or Greg's?"

Mac leafed through the pages until he found the P's, and the place where he had written her name. "See for yourself," he said, sitting down beside her.

"'One hot number,'" she read, then looked up at him with an eyebrow cocked. "Is that really what you thought of me?"

"It's what I still think," he replied, kissing her.

"I'm not sure how I feel about that."

"You should be happy. Because that's how this whole thing started. And love has to start somewhere."

She slipped her arms around him. "I'm just glad this is where love has brought us."

"Me, too." He kissed her again and whispered, "I love you."

"And I love you, too," she replied. "And because I do..." She ripped the page with her name out of the address book. Then she sent the rest of the book sailing across the room to the wastebasket beside the dresser.

From the doorway, Julianna protested, "You threw away a book!"

"It's okay," Hailey told her. "It's a little something your father will never, ever need again."

"Amen," Mac agreed.

Then he kissed her to seal the deal.

* * * * *

Silhouette's recipe for a sizzling summer:

* Take the best-looking cowboy in South Dakota
* Mix in a brilliant bachelor
* Add a sexy, mysterious sheikh
* Combine their stories into one collection and you've got one sensational super-hot read!

Summer Sizzlers

MEN OF Summer

Three short stories by these favorite authors:

Kathleen Eagle
Joan Hohl
Barbara Faith

Available this July wherever
Silhouette books are sold.

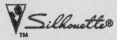

Silhouette®

TM

SS96

MILLION DOLLAR SWEEPSTAKES

SWP-M96

FORTUNE'S Children™

New York Times Bestselling Author
REBECCA
BRANDEWYNE

Launches a new twelve-book series—FORTUNE'S CHILDREN
beginning in July 1996 with Book One

Hired Husband

Caroline Fortune knew her marriage to Nick Valkov was in
name only. She would help save the family business, Nick
would get a green card, and a paper marriage would suit both
of them. Until Caroline could no longer deny the feelings Nick
stirred in her and the practical union turned passionate.

MEET THE FORTUNES—a family whose legacy is greater than
riches. Because where there's a will...there's a wedding!

Look for Book Two, *The Millionaire and the Cowgirl*,
by Lisa Jackson. Available in August 1996 wherever Silhouette
books are sold.

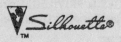

Silhouette®

You're About to Become a

Privileged Woman

Reap the rewards of fabulous free gifts and benefits with proofs-of-purchase from Silhouette and Harlequin books

Pages & Privileges™

It's our way of thanking you for buying our books at your favorite retail stores.

PROOF OF PURCHASE
YT-PP152
Offer expires October 31, 1996

Pages & Privileges ™

**Harlequin and Silhouette—
the most privileged readers in the world!**

For more information about Harlequin and Silhouette's PAGES & PRIVILEGES program call the Pages & Privileges Benefits Desk: 1-503-794-2499

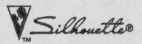

Silhouette®

YT-PP152